THIS CASE STUDY BELONGS TO:

_____

THE SECRET OF ANIMALVILLE

Richard Mueller

Original concept by
David Simons
Artwork by
Egidio Victor Dal Chele

SHANGRI-LA PUBLICATIONS
WARREN CENTER, PENNSYLVANIA

ZOONAUTS ™: The Secret of Animalville
ISBN 0-9719496-6-2, LCCN 2002010779

Copyright © 2003-2004

David Simons

ZOONAUTS ™ is based on original characters by David Simons and Cathy Lynn,

We wish to thank NASA for the use of their public images, and for pictures of 'Mickey' the Senagal Gray Parrot, provided by her owner Ellen Uittenbogaard, and lastly, the word "ZOONAUTS" is the creation of Sheldon Lee Gosline.

Edited by Sheldon Lee Gosline, Proofed by Cathy Lynn

Published by PANDA PRINT
A division of **Shangri-La Publications**
3 Coburn Hill Road, Warren Center PA
18851-0065 USA, TEL:866-ZOO-NAUT

PRINTED IN CHINA

Library of Congress Cataloging-in-Publication Data
Mueller, Richard, 1946-
  Zoonauts : the secret of Animalville : a novel / by Richard
Mueller ; original concept by David Simons ; edited by Sheldon
Lee Gosline.
    p. cm.
  Summary: The animals on Earth develop super abilities and
pursue their mission to save the planet from Amadorians, hostile
invaders from a distant galaxy.
  ISBN 0-9719496-6-2 (alk. paper)
  [1. Science fiction.] I. Simons, David, 1936- . II.
Gosline, Sheldon Lee. III. Title.
  PZ7.M8788Zo 2002
  [Fic]--dc21

                                    2002010779

For Orders Call: **866-ZOO-NAUT** (866-966-6288); **ZOONAUTS**™ is a trademark of Shangri-La Publications

DEDICATED

TO

CODY SIMONS
AND
BRYAN ROY SMITH

ZOONAUTS

A Note to the Parents Among You

We take many liberties in our storytelling. *ZOONAUTS: THE SECRET OF ANIMALVILLE* is no more a history of NASA animal research and space exploration than *HARRY POTTER* is a treatise on ceremonial magic, or *THE HOBBIT* is an instruction manual for the slaying of large red dragons. Bearing that in mind and have fun!

This book is the record of Jen and Cody Stroud, for all Earth children like Sara to learn about Animalville. It concerns a war lasting centuries, but only since the NASA Space Program has Earth had a chance to fight back. This war may go on for years. We may win or lose, but no one will say we did not try.

"We need another and a wiser and perhaps a more mystical concept of animals. Remote from universal nature, and living by complicated artifice, man in civilization surveys the creature through the glass of his knowledge and sees thereby a feather magnified and the whole image in distortion. We patronize them for their incompleteness, for their tragic fate of having taken form so far below ourselves. And therein we err, and greatly err. For the animal shall not be measured by man. In a world older and more complete than ours they move finished and complete, gifted with extensions of the senses we have lost or never attained, living by voices we shall never hear. They are not brethren, they are not underlings; they are other nations caught with ourselves in the net of life and time, fellow prisoners of the spendour and travail of the earth."

From *THE OUTERMOST HOUSE*
by Henry Beston

The Secret of Animalville

Preface

Fishwick and Kornblend were not happy Amadorians as they reached the Supreme Palace of Amador, under the poisonous yellow sky.

Calling it a palace was a kindness, though it was certainly large enough. A big ugly rock pile, it reared up against the smoky skies. Amadorian emperors and warlords had been adding to the thing for centuries with no thought to design. The result was a lumpy great building as ugly as any in the galaxy, surrounded by a low and disreputable city, thick with smoke and machine noises. It was a strip-mall kingdom on a slum of a planet.

The palace's interior was no better than outside. The decor was a cross between a deserted fabric warehouse and closed steel mill. Martial banners with silly slogans hung amid rust and disrepair. Fishwick and Kornblend had been here many times and were used to it. They strode down the corridor, dragging their fat tails.

Amadorians all look a bit like dragons, though Fishwick was the taller and sneakier of the two. Kornblend's squat brutishness marked him as the tough guy. They were dressed in shoddy Amadorian fighter pilot gear with uniform insignia.

ZONAUTS

Above them, a robot eye swiveled about to find them. It did not seem very amused. Tre-Pok's voice suddenly blasted out from all sides. "Fishwick! Kornblend! Get in here!"

The doors to Tre-Pok's Strategy Room flew open. Fishwick and Kornblend stumbled in, tripped over their tails and went down in a heap. Untangling themselves, they staggered to their feet as Tre-Pok screamed, "Get up!"

The two pilots saluted, Roman-style, thumping their chests. "Yes, Your Awfulness!"

Tre-Pok glared at them. He was huge, a great scaly dragon with vestigial wings. He was impressive and he knew it. Looking down he examined the two pilots as if he had found them on his boot. "I've got a job for you two mouth-breathers. I want it done right!"

"Yessir!"

"Silence! You're using up my air." Tre-Pok stalked to his command console. Fishwick and Kornblend trailed fearfully behind him. Suddenly a screen lit up with a picture of a big blue marble, the planet Earth. Tre-Pok gave a satisfied grunt. "I want you to go to the Earth..." He rounded on them. "I trust that you remember where it is..."

The two pilots nodded vigorously.

The Secret of Animalville

ZOONAUTS

The image of Earth suddenly faded into one of the unsuspecting Zoonaut.

"Bring back this creature, the dog, Laika. You will bring her back alive and well."

"Alive and well..." Kornblend repeated. Fishwick elbowed him. "Ow," Kornblend went on. "How do we find her, Your Fearfulness?"

Tre-Pok's mad response frightened them. "Use genetic sensors we provided you!" He scorned them quaking in their boots. "If you succeed, you'll get medals and another stripe. Otherwise, when I vacation next, you'll be my luggage."

The two saluted so hard they almost broke their breastbones. "Now, get out of here!" Tre-Pok screamed. The two ran out immediately.

Tre-Pok scowled after them, not seeing the curtains move behind him as the High Rotocaster slipped into the room. He was a skeletal, spooky dragon. "This had better work..."

Tre-Pok nodded, but Rotocaster's attention was on the picture of the Zoonaut Laika. "I must find their weaknesses..."

The Secret of Animalville

One: Methuselah's Tale

"That was a VERY creative story Jennifer Stroud, but I think we have heard enough right now about Amador and silly space dragons!" interrupted Mrs. Patruski, the eighth grade English teacher. "You were SUPPOSED to have written a story involving something that happened to your family, not science fiction, or worse, fantasy."

"But..." began Jen. Mrs. Patruski waved her to silence.

"If I give the whole class an assignment, I expect ALL of you to do it. This assignment was not just about writing anything you feel like writing." She glared at Jen, who was trying to hide her anger, embarrassment, and urge to say something that would only make it worse.

Mrs. Patruski made Jen nervous enough that she sank back into her chair without a word. It was already turning into a bad spring term and still only February. She just knew what Cody would say when she got home, "I told you so", "how could you be so dumb? When are you going to learn?". Even though he was three years younger, he always had a better sense of what 'outsiders' could understand about their strange family. It made it so hard to have any friends when you couldn't tell them anything about home.

Truth is, no children had ever grown up in the kind of family as the Strouds. While their non-human nursemaids took care of them and taught them things no human children had learned, Jen was getting tired of telling other girls that they couldn't visit her at home. Oh, sure, she went to their places, but usually with some animal, watching everything she did. She felt like she was being spied on. It was too much to bear. Jen was deep in gloom as she left school that day.

"What was that weird story all about?" Sara, her best friend, burst into Jen's private reflections.

"Oh, just something Methuselah the parrot told me," Jen heard herself blurt out, before realizing what she was saying.

"You're bonkers Jen! Next you're gonna' tell me you know why the space shuttle Columbia blew up right here, over Texas!"

"Oh Sara..." with that Jen started crying harder than she ever had before. "It's just awful! I've just gotta' tell somebody or I'll burst ... Can you keep a secret? I mean a REAL secret. Not just something dumb?"

"Of course silly, dah!"
Jen started to pull herself together, realized that telling Sara anything was not only dangerous, but

useless too. She had to show her! "Sara, I need to tell you something, but can't. I need to let you in on the secret of Animalville, but don't know how. Let's go find Methuselah. He's real smart and may have an idea."

Sarafina Flores-Abaroa just knew that Jen had had too many moon pies for lunch. It was probably a sugar high, she told herself.

Just then Jen's mom pulled up. "Ready Jen", Mrs. Stroud called out.

"Where's our regular driver mom?"

"He's on a special mission today dealing with the crash," she whispered.

"Oh mom, can't Sara come home today? There's no one around to report us."

"You know the rules Jen!"

"But mom!"

"No, and that's final."

"Then let me walk home, so we can spend more time together", Jen pleaded.

"OK, but don't be too late!" and with that she drove away with Cody.

"Jen", Sara confided, "don't feel too bad. At least you have a real family. Grandma Camille is all I have, since mom ran off to 'find herself' in Utah. Anyway, she doesn't understand half of what goes on since she only speaks Spanish."

ZONAUTS

Jen remembered how hard it had been to communicate with Sara's grandmother, Camille Flores, whenever she visited, but the authentic Mexican food was great! "I know, but sometimes they are just too 'real'. They always watch us."

"I guess they love you", Sara almost whispered, "I wish I had that."

The two girls said almost nothing as they walked on through the quiet streets near the edge of town. The streets turned into a paved two-lane road. There, past the last house, squatting behind its fences, lay Animalville. A huge statue of Texas Bob cast its long shadow across the road, the military guard shack, and a tunnel where the road disappeared. Jen used the road every day, but none of her friends had, not even Sara. Jen indicated a stand of shady cottonwoods. "Wait for me there, Sara. I'll be right back."

"Okay," Sara said, sitting under a tree and watching Jen wave to soldiers in a guard shack and disappear down a tunnel. About ten minutes passed. Sara was starting to get nervous, when Jen's brother Cody showed up from nowhere.

"Oh, its you! Say, what's wrong with Jen?" Sara interrogated Cody, shaking off her surprise at seeing him. She fancied herself a secret agent, but had no idea how close she was to learning a real Top Secret.

"Nothin', what you mean?"

"She told some crazy science fiction story about another planet with dragons. She said something weird about it being by your parrot, then burst into tears!"

Cody rolled his eyes, as only a nine-year-old younger brother can, "Women! Now we're in for it!" Just then, Jen rounded the corner with Methuselah perched on her shoulder. Sara eyed the old bird, suddenly nervous. What if Jen WAS telling the truth?

"What have you done Jen?" Cody cried. "I told you they wouldn't understand about Amador. I told you so!" With that, Cody disappeared into a tunnel, like the white rabbit in *ALICE IN WONDERLAND.* The guards totally ignored him. They'd seen the Stroud kids argue before. The two girls looked knowingly at each other. Jen was right about at least one thing; her brother Cody was a pain.

Then, as far as Sara was concerned, the impossible happened. Methuselah spoke! Not just parrot-speak, but like a real human!

"Jen, Cody is right! Your Amador report was a big mistake!" Keenly sensing her amazement, Methuselah turned to Sara. "Excuse me, Sara, given lingual gifts, the other animals here in Animalville chose me

13

to be our spokes-being. What I am about to tell you is of course a top secret: a military secret. Do you know what that means?"

Sara stared at him, google-eyed, still not believing it, and nodded dumbly.

"Good," Methuselah went on. "Because with that secret comes the responsibility of never telling anyone else. If you do, terrible things could happen to Jen, to you, to all of us. So if you don't want to know..."

Sara was excited beyond words. She was scared. Her mouth was dry. She was totally amazed by Methuselah. She wanted to know this secret more than anything in the world.

She nodded. "I-I-I won't t-tell anyone," she said. "I want to know."

"Very well," said Methuselah. "This is a report about a war between Earth and Amador. I will tell you the story of how Animalville came to be, for I am older than most anyone. I remember these things. I know how we came here and how we are saving the world."

"You'll never look at animals the same way again. But you will listen hard, waiting for one of us to speak in your language, and you know what? We just might."

"You mean that there are other talking animals besides you!" Sara exclaimed.

"Of course!" Interrupted Jen, "You won't look at the sky the same way either, because there are things up there, flying just above our heads that did not come from Earth. Strange creatures from another planet are waiting to conquer us ... just like I said in my paper!"

"Excuse me, but I was giving this lecture Jen," Methuselah pointed out in a disturbed tone.

Sara was more than a little shocked, "Who else knows about this?"

Methuselah puffed out his feathers, tipped his head back, gathered his thoughts. "Well, the President, Air Force, NASA and other special people. Some are humans, others are dogs, cats, birds, mice, monkeys, gorillas, pandas; even koalas. I realize this is a lot for you to understand all at once, but..."

"You're not kidding?!" Sara exclaimed.

Methuselah chuckled. "Have you ever heard a parrot talk like me?"

"Well..ll...no."

"Please get comfortable. I will tell you a story so amazing you may not be able to sleep. In fact, you may never want to sleep again."

Jen and Sara rested under a tree by the fence that surrounded Animalville. The day was cool and sunny. Breezes ruffled the grass, but their attention was totally on the old gray parrot.

"After the last great human world war—called the Second World War—the world was left with two great and powerful nations; America, called the United States, and Russia, called for a time the Soviet Union, but now called Russia again. There were many other nations, but my story is about America and Russia—the Superpowers."

"Superpowers are large places with many creatures and resources. They distrust, envy, and consider each other evil. That is dangerous, for with terrible weapons, any war could become the last one. Humans were frightened, air raid sirens blew and children crouched under desks. They waited for terrible bombs. It was very frightening even though they called it something that sounded like a game, 'duck and cover'."

"I don't remember any of that," Sara said skeptically.

Jen added, "Wasn't it like our 'lock in place' drills? We started those after September 11th."

"Sort of, but not exactly. You were not born yet, but I watched and wondered if everyone had gone crazy. Maybe it's happening over again."

"How did we survive back then?"

"Luckily, there were a few sane humans." Methuselah continued, "It was called a 'Cold War' because it was potentially dangerous, like dynamite, which explodes if it gets too hot. Smart humans realized that if leaders weren't given something to do, they'd argue. We'd then have a Third World War. America and Russia needed to compete, but not fight. Olympics were nice, but only every four years. People forgot them almost immediately. There was culture, but while Russians had ballet, Americans had television, so that was out. They needed somewhere difficult, dangerous and far away to keep quarrelsome people very busy. With all lands discovered, 'Wild West' tamed, and 'Dark Continent' explored, there were no more mysteries here. Then a very smart human looked up and said, 'let's go to space'—a perfect answer. Up there are countless stars and planets to explore. But first people had to find a way to escape gravity."

"I know, we made rockets!" Sara exclaimed.

"Yes, but you humans had only been flying for about fifty years. During the Second World War—did I mention that I was in that war?"

"Not yet," Jen said with a yawn, "but I'm sure you will eventually. You always do."

"Yes, people flew over 40,000 feet up, over seven miles, but space is millions of miles. They needed a new way to fly. You are right Sara, they picked rockets, but they weren't safe. Humans decided to first send animals. If we died, they could try again, but if we lived, you would follow.

ZONAUTS

This sounds cruel but dogs, cats, horses and even birds had been helping humans for thousands of years. We are used to sharing dangers. Dogs protect your flocks, cats keep houses free from rats, horses carry you, and birds deliver messages and sing for you. When humans began sending us animals into space, animals were afraid, but also proud. Something in space also changed us forever. At first, you humans didn't notice."

"How do you know all this?" Sara asked.

"Simple," Methuselah said, winking a dark eye. "I was the first animal to change, although I was never in space. When the space program started, I was already over thirty. They said, 'Methuselah, you are too old,' so I lived at the Cape Canaveral base, then at Houston, and watched other animals go into space."

The Secret of Animalville

Two: A Smart Old Bird

Sara was getting more curious about this strange old bird, "How old are you anyway?"

Methuselah puffed out his feathers with pride, "I am over eighty now. 'Methuselah' is a name that means very old. It's true. Look it up."

"But how exactly did you change?"

Methuselah's eye gleamed, "As I said, I was never in space, because I was already too old for the space program. Aliens changed me in 1952! But my story with humans started in 1944. I was already in my twenties and living in a West African jungle, in Ghana. I am a Senegal Gray Parrot, named after the Senegal River. We are smart birds, though I was going to get a lot smarter. First, I did something very stupid."

"What?" asked Sara, all ears.

"There was plenty to eat in the jungle, but on the edge there was a large town with a flat clearing called an airport. It was the US Army Air Corps Base at Takoradi, but I did not know that then. Large airplanes came from the west across the Atlantic Ocean and landed there. Men did things to them and then flew east, never to return. I later found out they were coming to Takoradi from the United States by way of Brazil. They were heading east to Egypt, China and a war. The men in Takoradi were refueling and checking them to make sure they were fit to fly. Birds do these things naturally, but you humans are not designed to fly so you build airplanes. I never saw airplanes before, on the ground, only flying over the jungle. I was about to see a lot more, but right then I was only interested in plums...sweet plums...ripe, succulent, delicious plums."

"I don't see the connection," Sara admitted.

Methuselah elaborated, "There was a plum tree on the air base. I could see it from my jungle perch. It grew by a window of a building I later learned was the Aircrew Transient Barracks, where flight crews slept between flights. Humans can't perch in trees as we birds do. But plums, wonderful sweet plums; all I was interested in were plums. I determined that I must have them.

"I flew from the jungle, over a fence, and straight to the tree, where I ate the most wonderful plum. Deciding that this was good, I planned to do it every day. So I did, for ten days. I had not noticed that there were other plums missing beside those I had eaten. Humans like plums too, and the human who tended this tree, a Sergeant Otis Fox, had seen me fly there. He was able to trick me, for back then Sergeant Fox was smarter. When I flew to the tree the eleventh time, I heard a snapping sound, and Sergeant Fox caught me in a net. After then, I lived in a cage in his room of the Aircrew Transient Barracks."

"It must be awful to be in a cage," said Sara.

"Well," Methuselah replied, "there are worse things but it wasn't pleasant."

"Go on," Jen said impatiently. Methuselah shook his head. Human children are so impatient.

"Very well. Sergeant Fox was not a transient. He was in charge of barracks, and now he was in charge of me. I must admit; he treated me well. He made me stay in a cage, which I hated, but he gave me seeds and fruit to eat, even plums. He talked to me and got me to talk back to him, which is all I could do then, because that is what normal parrots do. I did not understand much, but I did say what he asked. After a time he clipped my flight feathers, so I could not fly away, and let me out of the cage. Sometimes I rode around on his shoulder while he worked. Other times he let me sit on a perch by his door."

"Wait a minute," interrupted Sara, "you can fly now... how come?

"Oh, my feathers grow back every year. Aren't birds great! Anyway, the men who flew planes, the aircrews, would talk to me, feed me and even get me to say things I shouldn't. I know now what those words meant, so I shall not repeat them to you, but I did not know then. Bad language sent me to China."

Sara giggled and Methuselah nodded. "I was sitting on my perch one day, chewing a plum. The General in charge came in. If I had known better, I would have never called him a 'fat-a**ed desk jockey.' Of course, I didn't know what that meant, but he did! His face turned red. He found Sergeant Fox and told him, 'Either that bird is off the base by sundown or YOU go to Greenland,' - not as nice a place as it sounds. Fox immediately gave me to a transient pilot, Major Mike McIntosh."

"Wait a minute," said Sara, "why didn't you just fly back to the jungle or somewhere?"

"My wings were clipped, remember, so I couldn't fly. I was back in a cage, in a B-29 bomber heading east to join the B-29 'High-Flying Floozie' crew. Don't ask what it is. It isn't nice."

"What isn't nice?" immediately asked Jen.

"Floozie, but I told you not to ask."

"I know what a floozie is," said Sara. "I saw it used in a movie once."

"At any rate," Methuselah said, quickly changing the subject, "the crewmen were good to me. I got to know them as we flew to Cairo, then Bombay and on to China. I missed my jungle, but was well fed and having adventures, so it wasn't bad. Besides, there are jungles in China too.

"The crew wanted me on their missions as their lucky bird, so the squadron armorer made an oxygen mask that just fit my beak. I looked dashing and could go high where there is no air. Flying from Africa to China we were low enough that we didn't need bottled oxygen. On these missions, we went up 30,000 feet (five and a half miles). I was the first parrot to fly so high. We flew a number of missions, had a few adventures and then the war ended. Major Mike stayed in the Army Air Corps, which soon became the US Air Force. I stayed with him."

Meanwhile…

In 1944, Germans, who we fought in WWII, developed a liquid-fuel rocket called V-2. Instead of using it in space, they shot explosive warheads at Great Britain, but still lost the war. The US brought back many V-2 rockets.

In 1945, White Sands Proving Ground for rocket research opened in New Mexico's desert.

In 1946, a US-launched V-2 rocket carried a spectrograph 34 miles high to study the sun.

In 1947, a US jet plane broke the sound barrier for the first time.

In 1949, a rocket test ground was set up at Cape Canaveral. At White Sands, the first two-stage rocket flew up 240 miles.

ZONAUTS

Three: Much Smarter

"But, how did you become so smart?" Sara asked. "Most parrots learn things like, 'Polly want a cracker,' or 'Who's a pretty boy?' But you..."

"Yes," Methuselah broke in. "I do have a considerably more extensive vocabulary...

"Fewer ten dollar words!" moaned Sara.

"OK, so I use big words, get over it! As for snacks, I prefer almond croissants or bearclaws. But, we were talking about intelligence, right? By 1950, a war broke out in Korea and Major Mike and his crew in the 'High-Flyin' Floozie II' (a new B-29 with the same name) were assigned to an island named Chengtu. I went with them. By then I had gone nearly half-way around the world and our crew had flown over 40 missions in two wars without anyone hurt, so they said I was their good luck charm. Everyone at the base visited me, even the General in charge, who I did not call any names. We flew photographic reconnaissance, meaning we flew over Korea to take pictures. We never dropped any bombs. I didn't think much about that then, but now I'm happy about it. I don't like the idea of killing, friend or enemy.

"We were flying back from the Yalu River after the crew took their pictures. Everyone was relaxed, when suddenly a hole appeared in the wall next to my cage; then more holes. A MiG was after us shooting (a MiG was type of enemy plane) so Major Mike put the 'High-Flying Floozie II' into a climb. We went up, higher, farther and faster than ever before. We lost the MiG in a cloud at about 33,000 feet (more than six miles up). That is when IT happened."

"IT?" Sara asked.

"Shhh," Jen whispered. "I love this part."

"The plane was flooded with bright yellow light, like it was coming from the walls. A crewman yelled that we were dead. That was all I remember, until later. When I awoke the plane was flying but I didn't hear the crew, so I opened my cage (which I had never been able to do before) and walked up to the cockpit, where they fly the plane. Everyone was asleep. When I looked out through the round window, I could see the ocean below. In fact, the ocean was much too close, so I perched on Major Mike's shoulder and banged my very hard curved beak on his forehead until he awoke. 'What the Devil!' he said, and 'Where are we?' Then he started to yell to wake the crew. Everyone ran to do things. Gradually we gained altitude and made it back to base. I returned to my cage, listened and..."

"Were you scared?" asked Sara.

ZONAUTS

"I was very scared! Suddenly I understood English. That yellow light did something. While it made us all sleep, it also boosted my brainpower. I had changed. I was smarter than most humans and smart enough not to tell. I continued to talk like a normal parrot, even when they gave me a medal for saving the 'High-Flying Floozie II' crew. Then war ended. Major Mike McIntosh, promoted to Lieutenant Colonel, brought me to the US."

Meanwhile...

In 1955, the US began the Vanguard project for launching artificial satellites.

In 1957, the Soviet Union launched its first artificial satellite, Sputnik I, and launched a second satellite carrying a live dog, Laika.

In 1958, the first US Vanguard satellite, pictured here, went into orbit.

In 1959, the Soviets put a satellite (Lunik) in orbit around the sun, and crashlanded a rocket (Lunik II) on the Moon. Lunik III then photo-graphed the dark side of the Moon. Miss Baker, a squirrel monkey, flew into space on a Jupiter rocket and returned safely to Earth.

Four: The Space Race

"Sara, do you remember the 'space race' I told you about?"

"Yes."

"When it started, Colonel Mike and I were assigned to it. At first Colonel Mike was assigned to fly B-29s used in launching rocket planes for test pilots, like Chuck Yeager. When that phase of testing was completed, he was reassigned from base to base. I learned that Colonel Mike's job was to organize experimental animals for a space program and supervise their human caretakers. I worried about this, because I had been reading Colonel Mike's magazines when he was out. I learned how animals were used to test medicines and cosmetics. Many animals were hurt. I read about hunting and people abandoning cats and dogs. This made me furious; depressed you might say. I stopped eating, talking, and even pulled out my feathers. Colonel Mike became very upset and fussed over me. He bought me sweet plums, special seeds and Brazil nuts. He talked to me and scratched my neck. That is when I realized a truth. Many people, like Colonel Mike, were good to animals. They love their pets and take great care of them. Some even go without food themselves to pay for medicine for

27

their dogs, cats or birds. Others arrange organizations to protect animals and volunteer at shelters or rescue societies. Humans can be very confusing. But since I was destined to live with them I decided to help the best of them and see what good I could do too. I can tell, Sara, that you're one of those good humans. That's part of the reason I'm letting you in on this secret."

Sara nodded, but didn't say anything else. Methuselah went on.

"Colonel Mike and I had been working with chimpanzees used to test gravity effects. They were strapped into machines called centrifuges and whirled around at great speed. That made them feel very heavy; the way I felt when Major Mike climbed very fast in our B-29. Many chimpanzees became sick. Some died. I thought that strange, because I had known chimpanzees back in Africa who were very strong. I began watching them while Colonel Mike was doing other things. They talked to one another from cage to cage. I realized they were lonely, needed to touch, groom and exercise. They felt as if they were in prison. I guess they were. I also realized that I understood their language."

"One day I began talking to them, but they got so excited at hearing a bird speak in chimpanzee that they all started screeching. The humans in charge came running to see what the problem was. I played dumb; acted like I had no idea. I tried to talk to them several times after that. For a long time, they got excited, screeched and shook the bars. Then one female named Sheba answered. First, all she asked was how I could speak their language. Finally, I found out what was wrong; no one let the chimpanzees be happy. They needed to groom each other, play and exercise. That was a big problem, for now I had to break the news to Colonel Mike."

"That night, after dinner and watching 'The Twilight Zone' on TV, Colonel Mike was sitting in his easy chair, reading about chimpanzee behavior. I was sitting on my perch, pretending to be interested in a Brazil nut. I was actually worrying about how to break the news to him that I could really talk. He might think he was crazy. You humans often think you're going crazy if something they can't understand happens. You might think they would study the new thing, but no, they like to blame themselves first. You are a confusing species!"

"Just then, Colonel Mike made it easy. He looked off into space and said, 'I don't know. I don't get it. We really know so little about animals.' He looked at me. 'You're a smart bird, Methuselah. What do you think?'

"About what, Colonel Mike?" I replied. His eyes widened. He dropped his book. He stared at me, and I realized that, without thinking, I had answered aloud. We looked at each other. I was (as far as I know) the first animal who had become as intelligent as humans and the first who could really talk. Colonel Mike was about to become the first human to know this. I had to be very careful so he wouldn't think he had lost his mind.

"'You can talk,' Colonel Mike said quietly. He sounded hoarse. I think he was frightened. I remembered the moment back in the B-29 when I first understood human speech; how frightened I had been. I knew what he was feeling."

"I told him that lots of birds talk."

"But not like you," Sara agreed.

"True, and that's the same thing he said. I looked at him, he looked back, 'Who are you?'

"'I'm Methuselah. You brought me here from Africa years ago.' I waited while this registered."

"'I haven't been drinking,' he muttered. 'I don't drink. Maybe I should start.' I should explain; some humans like to drink what they call alcohol. It makes them act foolishly. Their heads hurt later. I never saw much point to it. One crewman on the 'High-Flyin' Floozie' once gave me some beer. It tasted like dead beetles, left in a puddle of hot water much too long. I don't know what they see in it."

"Drinking is pretty awful", agreed Jen.

"Yes," added Sara, "It scares me when adults drink." They had talked about this before.

"Well, Colonel Mike was not drunk. He was quite normal. I tried to calm him. 'I'm different. I'm changed; much smarter than I was.' He asked, 'How smart?' I could answer exactly because I read his books and magazines when he was out. 'In human terms, I have an I.Q. of 145.'

"That's impossible!" Exclaimed Sara.

"...just what he said. Impossible – standard human reaction to anything you don't understand. How you ever learned to fly with that attitude is beyond me, but somehow you muddle through."

"Nevertheless," he replied, "It is true. For a couple of minutes we looked at each other. Then Colonel Mike began to test me, asking me a long string of questions... 'Who is the President?'

'John F. Kennedy.'

'What does NASA stand for?'

'The National Aeronautics and Space Agency.'

'The atomic weight of Cesium?'

"What is it?" asked Jen with a twinkle in her eye.

"I'm a parrot, not a chemist, but I could look it up if you like."

"Don't bother, we don't need to know until I take chemistry," said Sara to keep to the subject.

"Anyway, this went on for a while. First I thought he was trying to trap me, or figure out that this was a trick using a microphone and a speaker, like on CANDID CAMERA. Then I realized he was determining just how much I knew. Since I was a parrot, I clearly should not have had so much education. Finally, he sat back satisfied. 'You've been reading haven't you?'

'Yes.'

'Watching television? What about radio?'

'Yes.'

'What else?'

'I remember all I see.' Memory was my 'gift,' about which I will say more later."

"You didn't remember Cesium," Jen said smugly.

"That's true," Methuselah replied. "It's one thing to remember everything. It's another to organize it in your head to find it the moment someone asks." He raised a claw, scratched his head feathers, smoothing them back into shape.

"Then Colonal Mike asked me the big question. 'How did this happen?'

"'Remember the time when the bright light flooded the plane. We all fell asleep. When I woke you, I could understand what was being said.' Then I asked a question that had been bothering me for almost ten years. 'Didn't you change too? And the other men?'

"Colonel Mike seemed disappointed. 'No. I haven't. I haven't heard about the others, but six of them are still alive and I'll ask.' He did, but none of them had been changed. Just me."

"So humans don't change?" Sara asked. "Only animals?"

"Not as far as I know," Methuselah replied. "Oops! Awrrk. Polly wants a cracker. Pieces of eight, kiss the black spot!"

Sara was totally confused by this strange outburst, but Jen had seen it all before. It was the way Methuselah acted when a human who wasn't in on the secret of Animalville got too close. She turned to see the Air Force Sergeant from the gate ambling up.

"Hi, Sergeant Murphy."

"Hi, kids," Sergeant Murphy replied. Methuselah had fallen silent and was scratching his head with his foot. He looked like any other parrot, but kept a close eye on the Sergeant.

ZONAUTS

"Are you kids all right?" Sergeant Murphy asked. "It's just that you're usually in by this time of day." Jen glanced at the sun, sinking toward the horizon. The Sergeant was right. She shrugged.

"It was such a nice day, we thought we'd sit out and enjoy the weather."

"Hey, that's great," said the Sergeant. "I wish I had me a parrot but I don't think my cat would approve. You kids have a nice time. G'bye, Polly." He went back to the gatehouse. When he was out of earshot, Methuselah made a grumpy clicking sound. "Why do you humans insist on calling all of us parrots, 'Polly?' Really!"

Jen and Sara laughed until Methuselah fixed them with a stern look. "If there are no further interruptions ..."

"Go on," said Sara. "Please. I want to hear."

"Very well. I asked if Colonel Mike was going to tell NASA and the Air Force about me. Colonel Mike laughed. 'Not unless I'm bucking for a Section Eight.' A Section Eight is what the Air Force calls it when they ask a crazy person to leave."

"'Well, I don't think you're crazy,' I told him reassuringly."

"'That's not much of a comfort coming from a talking bird with an I.Q. of 145.'

"'Parrot,' I said, correcting him.

"'You're a parrot with an I.Q. of 145,' he said ruefully. 'My I.Q. is only 142.' He snapped sharply. 'How do you know it's exactly 145?'

"'I sent away for the tests,' I said sheepishly. 'I write too.' He shook his head; looked at the clock. 'It's almost midnight. Let's turn in. We'll talk more about this tomorrow.'

"**N**ext morning, Colonel Mike called in sick. We spent the day talking and drinking fruit juice, 'to keep our whistles wet,' according to Colonel Mike. It must be a human thing. My whistle works best when my mouth is dry, but I love fruit juice."

"First we talked about aliens. People had been seeing them since the Second World War or earlier. I did not know then what I know now about Amador, Amadorians, and their plans. If I had known, perhaps things would have developed faster, and Animalville would have come about sooner. Humans have a saying; 'there's no use crying over spilled milk.' That means, instead of worrying about what went wrong, start thinking about what to do right. Good advice."

ZONAUTS

"Since Russians, Chinese and Koreans had no weapon like what struck the 'High-Flyin' Floozie II,' we concluded that aliens must have done it. Colonel Mike studied something called Project Bluebook, an Air Force program about aliens."

"Meanwhile, I talked to animals and told Colonel Mike what they said. I began with the chimpanzees. Colonel Mike made important changes to improve Zoonaut care to make their lives better: better food, bigger cages, regular walks and other exercises. He was promoted from Lieutenant Colonel, to full Colonel, called a 'bird' because of eagles he wore on his uniform. I thought it was a funny title, but it was a promotion and honor. We settled in Cape Canaveral, Florida and worked full time taking care of animals."

"Colonel Mike wrote reports on animal behavior and conditions. NASA and the Air Force used these reports to improve lab animal conditions. He had less success finding out about aliens. After he asked too many questions, two men in dark suits called Mr. Valentine and Mr. Christmas, came to the house. They told Colonel Mike to stop asking questions or his career would be over and he would be in trouble. They did not know that I could understand everything. Up to this time, only Colonel Mike and a few other animals knew about me. We decided to keep it that way as long as possible. When I asked who

Zonauts

they were, Colonel Mike said that they were from NSA, which sounds like NASA, but instead is a security agency that tells you when to stop asking questions. By 1976, we made a great discovery."

Meanwhile…

In 1960, Echo, the first communications satellite was launched.

In 1961, Russian Cosmonauts Yuri Gagarin and Germon Titov became the first two humans to orbit Earth. Ham, a chimpanzee paved the way for Alan Shepard and Gus Grissolm to become the first and second Mercury astronauts in suborbital flights. They splashed down in the Atlantic.

In 1962, the US Mariner spacecraft reached Venus. John Glenn became the first American to orbit the Earth. The Telstar communications satellite was launched. Americans Scott Carpenter and Wally Schirra orbited the Earth.

In 1963, Russian Valentina Tereshkova-Nikolayeva became the first woman in space.

In 1964, the US Ranger 7 probe took 4316 pictures of the Moon.

In 1965, Cosmonaut Aleksi Leonov took the first space walk. Virgil Grissom and John Young rode the first two-man Gemini capsule. The Mariner IV spacecraft reached Mars.

In 1966, the Russian probe Luna X became the first to orbit the Moon.

In 1967, Americans Virgil Grissolm, Ed White and Roger Chafee died in the Apollo I spacecraft fire. Surveyor III landed safely on the Moon, and took pictures and soil samples. The American Mariner V and Russian Venera 4 probes visited Venus.

In 1968, three-man Apollo spacecraft began orbiting the Moon.

In 1969, with the words 'One small step for man, one giant leap for mankind,' Neil Armstrong became the first human to walk anywhere other than the Earth, when he landed on our Moon.

In 1971, Salyut I, the first space station for Russia, went into orbit. The Mars 3 probe landed on Mars.

In 1972, Probe Pioneer 10 launched. It was the first human object to leave the Solar System.

In 1973, American Skylab space station went into orbit... and stayed there until 1979.

In 1975, Russian Cosmonauts and American Astronauts carried out Apollo-Soyuz, as the first Russian-US joint mission.

Five: Not Alone

By now Sara was sitting down with a dazed look frozen on her face. It was all just too unreal.

"Sara", Jen interrupted, "are you OK? Would you like something to eat? You look pale."

"I guess so, but I know I'm never going to tell anyone about this or they'd lock me up!" Sara interjected, "I guess I am thursty."

Methuselah smiled, "Jen, be a good friend and go get us a snack... perhaps some fruit juice. Now, if I may continue", Methuselah said with a whistle; a parrot version of clearing his throat. Jen skipped away without a sound while Sara was preoccupied. The whole thing spooked her.

As if the parrot read her mind he continued talking, "Things started getting really weird. One day Colonel Mike was away in another part of the complex. I was sitting in his office, going through reports, when I heard typing in the next room. We kept an old typewriter there among cages, spare .equipment and boxes of paper. Someone was typing. The typest was typing very slowly, but WAS typing, one key at a time."

"I put down a report on 'Fruit Fly Reproduction in Weightless Environments' (humans will study anything) and peeked in the room. What I saw surprised me more than anything had since the yellow light hit me.

"There was a mouse on the keyboard, banging one key after another with his feet. He was concentrating hard as he hopped. He hadn't seen me, but there were a lot of words on the paper. Since I had never heard of a mouse writing a letter, I decided that it wasn't meant to be private. Since I'd learned quite a bit of mouse-speak over the years, I decided to speak up.

"I asked the little guy, 'What are you writing?' Instead of running away or trying to hide, the mouse turned and looked at me. 'I'm making a machine report of what I did,' he said. 'You humans seem to do it all the time."

"Of course I told him I wasn't a human. I said, 'I'm a bird.' I would have said Senegal Gray Parrot, but mouse-speak is a very primitive language. It has no such precise words."

"'You speak excellent mouse—for a bird,' he said. Then I realized what all this meant."

"'You saw it,' I gasped. 'You saw the yellow light."

"'I don't know what 'yeh-low' means,' the mouse replied, for mice cannot see color, 'but I saw a light. It was very big. It's all in the report,' he added smugly, as if he'd been writing papers all of his life. I took this as an invitation and sidled up to the keyboard. This is what the mouse had written:

The Secret of Animalville

MY TRIP UP HIGH IN THE AIR AND THE BIG LIGHT
by Biff, Mouse, Number 34Z798J

Twenty days past I went up in the rockety-candle for a trip to the high air to be a test mouse for the rocket humans. I wore a mouse-breathing suit and was kept from harm by rag straps and water bubbles. The loud rocket made me squash a little but not bad like a car wheel and then the noise stopped. I was very very scared but I came to no harm and after a time I started to float. This was caused by being far from the ground and it made me stomach-less and I spit up greasy juice in my suit. I did not like this part but the floating was good. Then the big thing happened. There was no window in my rocket to see out but a very big light came through the wall and I went to sleep. When I woke the rocket was floating down on something called a pear-shoot and I was no longer the same mouse. I was very smart now. I looked the same but when the humans came to give me tests I learned more of their words each day. Now I know almost everything they say but since I cannot talk human-speech I decided to make this word report on the machine. Biff

"'This is very good for a first effort,' I said.
"'First F-foot?' Biff asked. I explained, then told him that he was very lucky I saw his report,

not a human who didn't understand. They'd think it was a hoax, if he was lucky."

"'Lucky?' I explained to Biff about how humans sometimes cut open things they don't understand to see how they work. Biff went pale, then ran back into his cage and closed the door. 'Are you going to tell them about me?' he asked in a small frightened voice."

"'No. You'll be safe,' I promised. Then, taking the paper, I went to find Colonel Mike."

"That night I told Colonel Mike about Biff. We decided right away to find out just how many other animals had been changed. Implications were clear: aliens were still operating. Until we could find out who they were and why they were doing this, Colonel Mike insisted that aliens had to be treated as hostile enemies."

"'But why,' I asked, 'if everything they do to us animals has made us smarter and stronger?'"

"'Because they don't ask permission. They interfere in our world. No one asked you if you wanted to be smarter.'"

"'No one asked me if I wanted to be trapped and become a pet,' I replied, 'but you humans do that all the time. You make us your slaves, you do tests on us, you eat us. Need I go on?'"

"'Just as animals eat smaller animals, Methuselah. You know about the food chain. But that is how things are, how things have developed on this planet. Now someone from another planet wants to change all that. Until we find out why, we have to assume these aliens are just getting ready to eat us. All of us.' He turned away. We were both upset and I hated that, for Colonel Mike was my best friend. But what would come later would prove Colonel Mike was right. The aliens were out to eat us. It would take two visitors from China to make us understand.

"Colonel Mike brought Biff the Mouse home and replaced him with another one so laboratory humans wouldn't notice. We started improving Biff's command of English. Unfortunately, with his mouse mouth he could write and understand it, but couldn't speak well, so I had to translate anything he wanted said to Colonel Mike. An electric typewriter allowed him to write faster. Biff became quite a typist.

"Meanwhile, we checked other animals. Three other mice (Alpha, Beta and George), three spider monkeys (Rollo, Suzee and Joe), a squirrel monkey (Miss Baker), a chimpanzee (Caesar) and a dog (Professor Mutzie) had seen it. Apparently, not all animals had seen the 'big light'. Colonel Mike then began negotiating with the Air Force for

ZOONAUTS

a real home for animals that had served their country in space. At first, he got no support for a Zoonaut home.

"Fortunately, the Air Force was too busy with war in Vietnam to supervise our lab, so whenever Colonel Mike wanted to take an animal for a night or weekend, no one said he couldn't. The sight of his car packed with monkeys, a dog and I was soon routine. Sentries started calling him 'Dr. Dolittle,' which was fine with Colonel Mike, if we were left in peace. But life soon changed.

Meanwhile...

In 1976, the space probes Viking 1 and Viking 2 soft-landed on Mars and began sending back pictures.

In 1977, the long distance probes Voyager 1 and Voyager 2 were launched to study Jupiter and the outer planets. They carried messages of friendship, recordings of earth sounds and music to introduce us to any aliens they encountered. Earlier, Pioneers 10 and 11 had small metal plaques identifying their origin for any spacefarers that might find them.

In 1979, Voyager 1 discovered a ring around Jupiter. Skylab 1 space station fell back to Earth, landing in the Australian desert.

Six: Making Our Way

"By 1980, our dining room was Animal Central with six typewriters on the table for anyone who wanted to communicate. Everyone did, except Professor Mutzie, a French poodle not suited for typing. Monkeys became very polished at putting new sheets of paper in typewriters and unjamming keys. Someone usually was clacking away. After computers, this got much easier. Paper piled high and it was all Colonel Mike could do to keep up. Soon he began missing meals and losing weight. I had to speak up. One night after dinner, when he, Mutzie and I were sitting out back, I brought up the subject. The others were all inside watching 'Wild Kingdom.' I started, 'Boss, you need help!'

"He looked at me. 'What sort of help?'

"'You're a General now. Shouldn't you have some Lieutenants around to help?' He laughed.

"'Explain my dining room circus, chimps lined up at the bathroom, and mice playing board games. You even do my taxes each year. You would all be in danger. No,' he said, shaking his gray head. 'No one else can help.'

"Professor Mutzie barked a long dog-talk sentence. I cocked my head to listen. It was simply brilliant. I told him so. He wagged his tail.

"'What was that all about?'

47

"'Mutzie asked why we don't run an ad in the paper for an assistant; an animal behaviorist civilian, perhaps a robotics expert.'

"'Robotics expert?' General Mike puzzled. 'Why? What good would that do?'

"'Mutzie thinks a robotics expert might design a talk-box for the animals to use.'

"Wait a minuite," Sara said. "You mean you all talk? I mean, not just you, you're a parrot—"

"Yes..."

"But other Zoonauts; cats, dogs, mice...?"

"Gorillas, owls, and even orangutans... Yes," said Methuselah. "They do now. You've probably figured out you'll be meeting them soon."

Sara's eyes were as big as saucers. "And talk with them?"

"Yes."

"Wow!"

Methuselah laughed. "I'd say that sums it up pretty well."

"But how?" Sara asked.

"...a voder circuit, or mechanical voice box. It was Professor Mutzie's idea. He read every science magazine and was up on this stuff. I thought it might work from the start. It certainly would make things a lot easier for General Mike. I still remember that night. We sat still thinking, almost like right now. We sat as the sun went down over the Everglades. Finally he stirred from his chair and went to write the ad saying, 'Well, why not? The worst they can do is lock us up.'

WANTED: FOR TOP SALARY Animal behavior/veterinary/zoology expert to supervise special research animals for sensitive projects. Experience in psychology and philology helpful. Think differently and be changed by experience. **Lifetime career opportunity!** Also seeking expert in cybernetics/robotics. Send resume to McIntosh, General Delivery, Pasadena, Texas.

"I looked at the ad, studied it a while, and turned to General Mike. 'It's good, but why philology?'

"'The study of languages. Since they will be dealing with many different animals—'

"'I see,' I said. 'Pasadena, Texas?'

"'I just learned that Space Animal Research is moving a new Space Center in Texas.'

Meanwhile…

In 1980, Voyager 1 and 2 flew by the planet Saturn, finding two new moons.

In 1981, space shuttle Columbia made its first flight and in 1982, four more flights.

Seven: Best Friend Lost

At that moment, Jen reappeared from the tunnel, carrying a basket full of goodies. There were bottled fruit drinks for the two girls, fresh pineapple juice for Methuselah, and cheese and crackers for all. They tucked the feast hungrily.

"Now, don't spoil your appetite," said Methuselah. "It's only a few hours to dinner."

"Don't be a 'mom,' Methuselah," said Jen. "I've got one already. She's enough." Noticing the sad look on Sara's face, Jen added, "Don't feel bad. I'm sure your mom will come back soon."

"Yeah," said Sara. "I guess. Did your mom actually let you take all this food?"

"Sorta. I didn't ask. She was busy down at the clinic. Anyway, your grandma cooks the greatest Mexican dishes... a lot better than this bland army surplus stuff we get around here."

Methuselah threw a wing over his eyes. "Miss Jen, do you mean to say that you absconded with these savorous comestibles."

"Not really... but I'm not quite sure that I know what you're saying?"

Methuselah began the serious interrigation, "Did you take this food without asking first?"

"Well, maybe..." Jen confessed quietly.

Methuselah flapped about excitedly while squaking, "Terrific! I've become a bad influence."

"No, you've just become a drama queen," said Jen.

Sara starting giggling and soon they were all laughing uncontrollably. When they eventually settled down, Sara began filling in Jen on what she had missed, "Methuselah has been telling me the wildest story about how you got all the animals to talk. Is that really how you all came here to Texas?" She then snacked on some cheese.

Methuselah nodded. "Yes, we moved to Texas then, but not here exactly. General Mike managed to get us special quarters on the edge of the base, where no one would bother us. For a while, people came around to see the animals. We watched them carefully to see if anyone was sympathetic enough to tell our secret, and if anyone was snooping. No, on both counts. Everyone just ignore us. Things settled down."

"We had more help then. NASA assigned an administrator to the Animal Unit, Dr. Brooks Wagoner, a good man, whose ancestors came from the same part of Africa as me. General Mike let him in on our amazing secret because they had known each other for years. Dr. Brooks never seemed to get over it. He worried about everything: animals, and aliens. He worried that he didn't know the full story; that no one would tell him the full story. He mostly worried about how to account for everything to Washington—without really telling anything. He kept talking about 'sitting on a bomb'. Somehow, he came up with a little money each year to help keep the place running, but never enough. That is when we started marketing electronic toys and investing with the help of your father, Sara.

"What are you saying? My father knew about all of you!"

"Of course," Methuselah said, dropping the latest bombshell. Mr. Abaroa was the genius behind Abaroatronics, and our breakthroughs in computer circuitry became the basis for our current financial success. We also launched some of the top electronic toys and video games on the market. You know, like 'Robo-puppy' and 'Cyber-evolution.' I can't remember all the products. Mungo would remember of course, since he works on all the test versions."

Sara interjected, "Mungo? Who's that?"

"Another parrot," said Jen.

"Oh," Sara replied.

"But the important thing is that it made us financially self-sufficient," Methuselah said. "I can't tell you how much…"

"About seventy million dollars, so far," said Jen. Methuselah sighed.

The Secret of Animalville

"Another secret to keep," he said archly, eyeing Jen, who stuck out her tongue. "At any rate, for a while, we had a veterinarian named Dr. Marcuse, who had introduced your father's ideas to us, but he was killed in a car accident. Circumstances were mysterious, just like your father's recent 'accident'."

"So you don't think it was an accident?"

"I know it wasn't, Sara, they both knew too much about the secret success of Abaroatronics, its ties to us Zoonauts and our investments. Your father, always blamed himself for Dr. Marcuse's death, but I didn't know why, until recently. We'll talk more about this later."

"In 1985, General Mike hired a young couple, right from grad school, Thomas and Angela Stroud. They were perfect. We all liked them. As I (and later another parrot, Mungo, our communications chief) went on rounds with them to translate, I learned a lot. Tom and Angie Stroud (humans like nicknames) grew

ZONAUTS

up in the same Iowa farm town, were high school sweethearts, and went to university together."

Of course Jen knew this story by heart.

"The Strouds married right after they graduated. They loved all us animals too, though at times Tom has had second thoughts. 'I studied animal behavior,' he would say. 'These aren't animals. They're little aliens.' We laughed then, but should have been more worried.

"Angie Stroud always wore long pants or long dresses because she had terrible scars on the back of her legs. When she was twelve, lightning had hit their family barn. Angie had gotten all of the animals out of a burning building, but was caught under wreckage when it collapsed. Her father pulled her clear, but the scars never disappeared. When word of this got around, it touched us so deeply that we formed a pact. Each animal swore to die before allowing any harm to Angie or Tom Stroud. That also includes Jen and Cody, and now you too Sarafina."

"Wow," whispered Sara. Jen just shrugged.

"My dear friend General Mike was getting pretty old, but he still made all rounds himself, with me trailing along translating. It was a summer day in 1987. In the primate house, we were talking to Kongo, a young mountain gorilla who had come to us after a shuttle flight. He showed remarkable signs of intelligence and scientific ability. We didn't know just then how far Kongo could go, but he had learned sign language well. He and General Mike were having a lively discussion about aerodynamic vectors, or something else I didn't fully understand—Dr. Tom was also a pilot—when I heard the sirens go off. I flew to a window and looked out. The sky was very dark, and then I saw a large tornado coming toward the base. I flew back to General Mike and Kongo. We all sprang into action. Kongo herded the other primates (chimpanzees and monkeys — Kongo was the only gorilla back then) down cellar, while General Mike and I went to help Tom and Angie Stroud clear animals from the main lab. We all hurried down to the storm cellar and waited until the tornado passed. It missed our labs, but when it was time to leave, we found General Mike unconscious on the floor.

"We raced him to the hospital. He had had a heart attack. Angie, Professor Mutzie the Dog and I waited until we learned that he was going to be all right. Then Angie and Mutzie went home. It was against the rules, but I turned translations over to Mungo and sat up with General Mike in his room all night. The next day, when he was feeling better, we talked over everything we had done and seen together, from the moment he had bought me from Sergeant Otis Fox right up to the tornado.

"Three nights later, he told me, 'Methuselah, parrots live a very long time. I think parrots exposed to that alien yellow light live even longer. You are my best friend, and I'd guess I'm yours.' I nodded, unable to say anything. 'I will probably die before you. If that happens, you must promise me to go on and help care for the other animals.'

"'I promise, General Mike,' I said. 'But you're recovering. Doctor says you'll be okay.'

"'Yes,' he said, smiling. 'That's what they say.' He took a sip of water and then put down the glass. 'I'm feeling much better. I'll be back at work before you know it.'

"'Well, don't scare me like that,' I said. Then I added, and maybe it was the wrong thing to say, 'an awful lot of us are depending on you.'

"He looked at me and smiled. He looked very tired. 'I know, Methuselah,' he said. 'It's always been my greatest pleasure and honor to have worked with you,' which made me feel immensely proud. Then he closed his eyes and went to sleep. I waited to make sure he was breathing okay and sleeping soundly, then I sat down on the windowsill and slept myself.

"I awoke to a loud shrill buzzing. Suddenly the room was full of nurses, and a doctor with something called a 'crash cart.' While they worked on General Mike, all I could do was stand

and watch. Finally the doctor said, 'He's gone,' then he turned to me, exactly as if I'd been a human and said, 'I'm sorry. His heart gave out.'

Methuselah paused for a moment, lost in thought, remembering. Sara reached out and stroked his feathers. When he went on talking, his voice sounded hoarse.

"They say birds can't cry, but I wailed and wept bitter tears. No one stopped me when I jumped down on the bed to kiss him goodbye. They covered him and took him out. I flew into the night, alone. It was the worst moment of my life. I stayed in the woods for three days, which I had never done since I left Africa. I wailed, wept and mourned. Then I remembered, thought, and finally slept. When I woke, I knew General Mike was gone. There was an empty place in me that has never filled to this day. Finally, I returned to base. At the cemetery, I watched them fire rifles, fold a flag and lower General Mike into the earth. I vowed then and there to do what I promised him; to take care of all the other Zoonaut animals, as best as I could. In fact, I've been very lucky to get help from special humans like you two, Jen and Sara."

ZONAUTS

Meanwhile...

In 1983, space shuttle Challenger made three flights, and a fourth in 1984. Sally K. Ride was America's first woman in space.

In 1986, the space shuttle Challenger blew apart 73 seconds after launch, killing six astronauts and teacher S. Christa McAuliffe. This disaster almost ended the American space program.

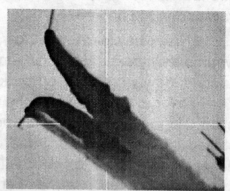

Mir (Peace) went into operation, becoming the first permanently manned space station.

Eight: The Strouds

"Because I spent so much time with General Mike, I hadn't gotten to know Tom or Angie Stroud well. Now I was suddenly working with them every day. I kept busy, to not think too much about missing General Mike. At moments, I still expected him to walk around the corner, smile and say 'let's get to work.' It made me very sad. Angie noticed but said that this was normal. She told me that I'd get over it. I guess I did, but I still miss General Mike. After all, I had known him for forty years. He would always be my best friend.

"There was a lot to do. Angie took care of the animals—we now had over a hundred; gorillas, chimpanzees, monkeys, lemurs, dogs, cats, rats, mice, toads, frogs, parrots, songbirds, owls, a raccoon, some snakes and whole colonies of insects. Not all had been into space of course, and the ones that hadn't were normal. The ones who had been in space had three things in common and all of them were remarkable.

"First, each of us became smarter. There was no way to tell how much smarter until we were tested. I had an I.Q. of 145. Mungo, a little green Senegal parrot who went into space in 1983, tested at 152 I.Q., but has no dignity to go with it. The most amazing one is Kongo the Gorilla, who

ZONAUTS

Tom Stroud tested. His I.Q. is close to 200. Kongo is so smart, that he and Tom are working on some secret projects. One involves investing in the Stock Market to solve our money problems – more later.

"The second thing was that we live longer, usually one-and-a-half times longer, which means I might see 2070, to really live up to my name! Professor Mutzie the Dog was 28 when he died and Biff the Mouse lived until he was 12. Something the aliens did made us much more efficient, smarter and healthier.

"There was a third thing, and that was certainly very alien. As each animal started to become mature—humans call it puberty—that animal developed a special power. Some powers became obvious immediately. The chimpanzee Ham III (born just after General Mike died and went into space two years later) could at first float, then levitate, and now fly. Kongo's daughter Patty Cake can move herself and other things with her mind. That is called telekinesis and psycho-kinesis. Kongo, besides being very smart, learned how to step outside of time. I know this sounds confusing but it will become clear later. Mungo the Parrot is a natural linguist. He can grasp any language he hears and speak it immediately.

The Secret of Animalville

"Naturally, with this many strange and wonderful things going on the Strouds decided these secrets had to remain truly secret. Only Dr. Brooks knew. He stays in Washington D.C., where the government is located and worries enough for all of us. Of course, no secret can last forever, and now I guess it is finally out!

"Now, as you know Sara, Tom and Angie Stroud had children of their own; Jennifer 'Jen,' born in 1992 and Cody, who was born in 1995. No children ever grew up with such nursemaids, as us animals to take care of them. We teach them things no human has learned since Tarzan (who wasn't real). You may wonder why I am telling you all this. Truth is, Sara, we need your help! Three things have happened; one good, one bad and one that will launch us all into our greatest adventure, but now it is getting late and you must go home. Don't tell anyone anything!"

Sara was visibly shaken back into reality. She looked pale! Had she been dreaming?

Jen felt responsible but lost for words, "I... I... well, life here in Animalville is always a surprise like that..."

"I thought we were friends Jen!" Sara babbled as she abruptly turned to go home, "How could you keep this all a secret from me?" Secretly though, she was glad to know something

61

about Animalville, her father and wanted to know more. What could Methuselah mean by saying they needed her help? Then turning around with a smile, "See you tomorrow!"

What Methuselah had said also confused Jen and she was ready to interrogate, "Why did you tell her so much?"

He only said, "Jen, some things are even a secret to you, but maybe I will let you know soon!" Then he flew down the secret tunnel and home for dinner. Jen followed after, under the watchful eye of Texas Bob, the monument to Animalville's past.

Meanwhile...

In 1989, Voyager 2 left our solar system. To teach any extraterrestrials about us, NASA placed ambitious messages about our world on both Voyager 1 and 2. The Voyager greeting, on a 12-inch 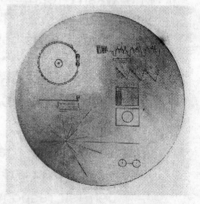 gold-plated phonograph, contains sounds and images of Earth's life and cultures. A committee, chaired by Carl Sagan, picked contents for NASA.

In 1990, Voyager 1 looked back from deep space and took the first photo of our solar system.

Nine: Fabulous Discoveries

Jen was unusually quiet at dinner that night. The tension with Cody was more than obvious, and Methuselah knew he had to do something soon.

He flew into Jen's room while she was pretending to do homework and started, "Need any help? Egyptian history is one of my favorite subjects… they worshiped birds you know."

"They also mummified them!" Jen retorted looking up over the edge of her book.

"Yes, a nasty practice of the late Graeco-Roman period, started by Greeks I recall."

Jen was not amused, "Don't get smart with me! You know exactly what I'm thinking about. It was one thing for me to open my mouth, but why did you have to go and spill everything?"

Methuselah lowered his voice, "We don't have much time left before they return. Things are happening faster since General Mike's death. I wish he could have seen these things, but…"

Jen interrupted, "You are babbling on, as usual. What is your point?"

Noticing a feather out of place and adjusting it with great dignity Methuselah continued, "I was just noting that many of you humans believe in a

63

place called 'heaven,' where people go after they die, and they can look down and see how the rest of us here are doing. I was simply reflecting. I don't know about this 'heaven,' but am certain he would be proud to see what we have accomplished. Especially the 'Mikes.'"

"What have the talking 'jelly beans' have to do with anything?" Jen asked in hushed tones.

"Kongo and Tom Stroud had been working on the problem of a universal translator for animals to speak to one another, in English, the only language we all know. While we never found a suitable robotics expert (Mungo claims that the ones who applied were all 'dweebs,' and that 'dweebs' talk too much, as if he didn't)..."

"And you don't know anything about that?" Jen interjected sarcastically.

Methuselah continued as if he hadn't noticed. "Kongo began experimenting with computer circuitry and managed to design what you call 'jelly beans,' electronic modules that many animals use to communicate. The correct term for these devices is 'Mike' (short for both microphone and for General Mike). Using simple surgery Angie Stroud implants this in the throat, attached to an animal's vocal chords, as small as a cat. Later, Kongo miniaturized it further for mice, toads and even for frogs. After an animal recovers from surgery, he or she can speak as well as Tom or Angie Stroud within days. Mungo and I didn't need them, of course, but Horace and Plato the Owls got them. Then all the other animals wanted them. Soon Angie was implanting them as fast as Tom and Kongo could churn them out. Communication became much easier but we had to continually caution some animals to not let themselves be overheard by other humans."

"Exactly my point!" Exclaimed Jen, "Why now, why is it different now?"

"I am getting to that, just let me fill you in on some details." Methuselah was clearly ruffled but shook his feathers back into place and continued, "It was during this time that I began writing a history of Animalville; involving everything that has happened since I met Major Mike, in 1944. Several other animals, including Horace and Plato, helped me. Soon we were filling up filing cabinets with reports, medical forms, test scores and pictures of each animal that had come through the program since NASA started. A special locked filing cabinet contained reports and essays written by animals themselves. If that were ever made public our secret would be out, so we use two keys to unlock it. I kept one, and Tom Stroud has the other."

"I'm still waiting…" Jen added sarcastically.

Methuselah continued, "Word of us already reached the wrong sort. The types of circuitry that we developed to go into the toys that Sara's father made – well, it was noticed. Some people saw the possibility of using this circuitry to build weapons, terrible weapons of mass destruction that could do harm to millions of people. Well, that's not what Animalville is about! So we have to keep these secrets from falling into the wrong hands."

"Wait a minute," said Jen. "Can't they just take apart the toys and figure out how the computer stuff works?"

"Good question, but no. It's not as simple as reverse engineering. We used techniques that could not be duplicated, but recently we've also started using materials that..."

"That what?" said Jen, getting excited in spite of herself.

Methuselah shrugged. "There's no way to say this so that it doesn't sound dramatic, so I'll just say it. We are using materials and technologies that are not of this earth."

Jen sat stunned for a moment. "That means–"

"Amador," said Methuselah. "May I go on?"

"OK, you've got my attention now!"

"Good... Our labs are a nice place, with animals eating, chatting, making new friends and discoveries. What you don't know Jen is that not all animals here were happy. Two in particular, Chuma a Chimpanzee and Bandit a Raccoon, always caused trouble. They complained. They wanted things changed. Then they wanted them changed back, just to get their way. Worse, they were thieves, stealing from other animals and you Strouds. While most animals don't collect things like humans, each of us had a few gift keepsakes. For example, Suzy the Orangutan had a favorite hairbrush. When she noticed it was missing she told me. I already heard complaints from several other animals, so Kongo and I went to see Chuma and Bandit. When we arrived, Chuma was sitting on his favorite seat, an old reclining chair, watching Bandit make a house-of-cards."

"'What do you two want?' Chuma said crossly. Neither Chuma nor Bandit had yet received a 'Mike,' so the conversation was a mix of languages, all of which I spoke.

"Kongo was not put off, 'Suzy's hairbrush, Horace's glasses, Mungo's autographed picture of Bruce Springsteen, and all the other things you've stolen. We want them back, now.'

"Chuma jumped up, ready for a fight, which would have been a mistake as Kongo is very strong, but Bandit the Raccoon waved his arms.

'There's no call for that,' he said. 'After all, we're all animals here. It's not like we're humans.' He said it with a smile, but it was plain that he meant to drive a wedge between the animals and humans. Kongo was not having any of that.

"'Humans are animals as well,' he said. 'They just evolved differently. If we are to survive on this planet, we had best make our peace with them. Besides, there isn't a finer bunch of humans than the Strouds.'

"'And General Mike,' I added softly. Even Chuma and Bandit lowered their eyes then. None of the animals would criticise General Mike. He had done too much for us. But Chuma grunted and Bandit was not to be convinced.

"'You have no proof we stole those things,' he said, his long raccoon tail lashing furiously. 'What would we want with pictures, eyeglasses and such junk? We have no use for them.'

"Kongo gave Bandit a fearsome stare. 'I believe you took them just to cause trouble. I hate to say this, but Tom and Angie have to know.'

"This was a dire threat because it meant other animals would find out. Chuma and Bandit glared and stood their ground. Kongo and I went to find Tom Stroud, who decided to talk to the two suspected thieves the next day.

The Secret of Animalville

"When the next day came, Chuma and Bandit were gone. Somehow, they escaped the base, leaving behind everything they had stolen— broken, torn or otherwise ruined—with a note saying that they hated us all and that they were going where they would be appreciated. What we didn't notice at first was that a number of our experimental computer circuits were missing too, along with a large file of our investment plans.

"The Space Center was on the edge of Houston, a big city. I wondered where they could have gone. Bandit could blend in with the local raccoons, but Chuma was a chimpanzee. He'd be conspicuous. But I was busy and soon forgot the entire business. My attention was on writing our history, which was about to get a lot stranger."

"Stranger," Jen repeated, "What do you mean 'stranger'? I still don't understand why you are letting Sara know so much.

"See, in addition to Zoonaut medical information, Kongo and had compiled massive amounts of research data on both computer circuitry and the Stock Market. Since Sara's father was so important in developing what we know, she can help us fight them. I am certain that Sara can help us in other ways too..."

"But it makes no sense! Why Sara?"

ZONAUTS

"Don't worry, I know what I'm doing. It's all part of the plan", said Methuselah in a tone that made it possible for Jen to go to sleep without worrying about it too much.

Sara's Grandmother Flores hardly noticed that she was late. That night, Sara had the weirdest dream. Jen and Cody were lost in a swamp with a bunch of animals. Smelly monsters were chasing them all. They tried hiding out in some roadhouse but nearly got caught there. She woke up in a cold sweat and couldn't remember much except that the only way Jen survived was by one of the gorilla's using some kind of mind control against the monsters. At school, the next day, Sara told Jen the whole thing, but neither girl knew at this time how useful that information was going to be.

Meanwhile...

In 1991, the Probe Galileo flew through the asteroid belt.

In 2003, the Space Shuttle Columbia broke apart while re-entering earth's atmosphere over central Texas. NASA warned about contaminated debris. Department of Homeland Security said there was no sign of human terrorism.

Tragic fall
Shuttle Columbia lost during descent

Shuttle flight path

Shuttle breakup

Palestine

Texas

500 MILES

Houston

Kennedy Space Center

Fla.

70

Ten: Busted!

Methuselah continued his history, writing into a carefully shielded computer file as follows:

As I told Jen, no secret lasts forever. Sara was certainly not the first outsider to learn about the Zoonauts. Remember that visit from Mr. Valentine and Mr. Christmas. General Mike and I were always worried that the wrong government people would find out about our secret and we would be split up, studied, poked and prodded, maybe even cut open to see how we worked. As year after year passed nothing happened, so we started feeling safe.

There was a war in a place called Iraq (it's also been in the news recently) so the government was busy again. We went on writing our reports and teaching animals to talk through their 'Mikes'. We gathered information about aliens. That was difficult since we had never seen any.

Then one sunny fall day in 1992, everything changed. We never learned how they found out, but that morning I happened to be looking out the window as trucks appeared, dozens of them, with HummVees, ambulances and even an armored car. They surrounded our labs and soldiers with guns got out. One man with a loudspeaker called for Dr. Tom Stroud to come out. Tom told me to

71

keep all the animals calm. Then he went out to talk. Meanwhile I, Kongo and Angie rushed around assuring each animal that it would be all right, and not to talk in English.

Then Tom returned; his face white. He said, "all the animals are being transferred. I don't know what is going to happen, but we should all cooperate and everything will be fine." He promised it would.

The trucks backed up and each of us was led into a sealed, darkened cage. I know how afraid some of the animals were, thinking that we would be cut open or even eaten, but everyone did as Kongo and I had asked. There was no trouble. This was a good thing, because the humans were all armed with guns and looked very serious. I just concentrated on General Mike and the other good humans I had known. I hoped that there were good humans among the men who were now leading us into cages.

When the cage became dark, I thought about this for a while, but then like all birds who are placed into darkness, I slept. We were moved several times—at least I was because I didn't see any of the other animals. However, I thought I heard Mungo singing a few times. They fed me. I don't know how long it was, perhaps even a day and a half. Finally, they interviewed me.

The Secret of Animalville

Three men in white coats asked me many questions. As in that first conversation with General Mike, I realized that they were first testing my intelligence. Those questions were simple. Then one of them took a 'Mike' out of his pocket and put it on the table. For a terrible moment, I was afraid that they had cut open one of us to get it. Then I noticed it was incomplete, and realized it must have come from the electronics bench where Kongo and Tom built them.

"What can you tell me about this?"

I cocked my head to one side. "Well, it's some sort of electronic gizmo I'd say. Not my field, actually. History, geography, philosophy—"

"Methuselah. That's fine. Enough." The one who said that had a thin smile. I didn't like his looks. "We know what it is."

"Then why are you asking me?"

"We want to know who made this and how they learned to make it."

"Whu-whu-well, I didn't do it," I said, imitating Jimmy Stewart in the movie *HARVEY*, one of my favorites. Two men laughed, but not the one with the thin smile. He glared at the other two, then me. He plainly had no sense of humor.

"Very funny. Did Tom Stroud make this?"

"Tom Stroud is an animal behaviorist, not a...a gizmo maker."

"What do you know about a company called Abaroatronics?" I said nothing.

"We know you have been making financial investments with their assets."

For a moment I was thrown off guard, "No that was Kongo...oops." I had said far too much!

The thin-lipped man pressed on. "We have plenty of evidence that Abaroatronics is using technology that is, at the very least, revolutionary. That technology originated in your research facility... a government research facility. Now, we want to know about it."

I said nothing, because I had nothing to say. "If you withhold information from a United States Government inquiry, you can be cited for contempt." I blinked at him, not completely sure what he meant by contempt. "That means," he continued, "it will be a very long time before you see any of your friends again."

That did it. I had had enough. "I'm saying nothing more without my mouthpiece," I squawked. "Get me a lawyer."

The thin-lipped man got red in the face. "You can't have a lawyer, you're a bird!"

"I have an I.Q. of 145," I bellowed. "What's your I.Q?" Then I added, "if you can hold me in contempt, I deserve to be represented by counsel. Get me a lawyer!"

The three men went into a huddle and began arguing among themselves. Finally the mean one with the thin smile stamped out of the room. The other two looked at me. "Excitable, isn't he?" I asked.

"Yes," one said nervously. "You can go back now. And thank you for your help."

They escorted me back to my solitary cage where I grumped and complained to myself until I fell asleep. I knew we were in trouble. I just didn't know how we were going to get out of it.

The answer came the next day when my covered cage was moved again. An hour later, they let me into a room without windows and just two doors. My friends, Tom and Angie Stroud were already there. I also recognized Dr. Brooks, Kongo, Mungo, Suzy the Orangutan and two dogs, Emma and Belle. I was not my usual calm self. "What's happening?" I blurted. "Are the others safe? Are we being tried? Where's our lawyer?"

"Lawyer?"

I told them about the three men in white. Tom shook his head. "They had no right to say those things. They were just trying to provoke you. The people we really have to convince are members of the Senate Sub-Committee on Intelligence." I knew what that meant, having discussed it several times with General Mike. They handled all of the spy stuff and secret programs for the government. We were certainly a secret program, though I didn't realize that some of us would also become spies.

I looked at the other animals. Emma and Belle looked morose. Mungo was his usual cocky self. Suzy was looking around, taking in everything. I was mostly worried about Kongo, especially since my confession. He looked stolid and thoughtful, like a huge boulder, but I knew from experience and the glint in his eye that he was getting angry, a long slow burn of anger that could erupt like a volcano. Theoretical physicist, super-gizmo designer and financier or not, Kongo was still a gorilla. Angie stood near him, her hand on his great hairy shoulder. She was whispering something to him—probably asking him not to break out the building wall—he was nodding, little bobs of his head, but his eyes were still red with rage. Tom and Dr. Brooks Wagoner were talking quietly when the door opened and a man in a suit stuck his head into the room. He hadn't expected to see so many uncaged animals, and swallowed hard before saying, "Dr. Wagoner. You and your party may come in now."

We trooped into the room and found seats at a long table. At least Tom, Angie and Dr. Brooks sat. Suzy sprawled in a chair with her feet in her lap. The two dogs stood behind with Kongo and Mungo. I perched on the table. On the other side of the room were five men in suits, the Senators. A uniformed policeman with a gun stood at each door. Dr. Brooks cleared his throat and gestured toward the police. "This is a Senate hearing. Do we need to have armed guards?"

An older Senator waved a hand in the air. "If you have these dangerous monkeys in here—"

He was interrupted by a fearsome grunt. Then Kongo spoke up. His voice was calm and controlled, but I could hear the underlying anger. "Senator, I am not a monkey, I am a 300-pound mountain gorilla. When angered, I can move fast enough to cross this room in less than three seconds. You'll need bigger guns if you're going to treat us this way."

The Senators looked as if they just heard the most amazing thing in their lives. I guess they had. They stared; mouths open. Finally, a young man spoke up. "Dr. Stroud, that's an amazing trick. How did you do it?" Then Dr. Brooks said the first funny thing I ever heard him say.

"He didn't. The parrot is a ventriloquist."

Mungo laughed. Eventually, all the animals, Tom and Angie Stroud, the Senators and guards began laughing. As the laughter died away, Kongo said—and he was almost smiling—"I do believe that that is what is called 'breaking the tension.' Gentlemen, my name is Kongo." Each of the animals gave introductions, and the Senators told us their names. I knew politics from often reading newspapers. They were powerful men and could affect our lives in a major way. We had to be careful. They already knew some of our technological and investment activities.

We were careful. The meeting lasted all day. They interviewed each of us. There were questions about General Mike, our experiments, the 'Mikes' that allowed us to talk, Abaroatronics, and the technology behind the new toys that were flooding the market as a financial success. Though some Senators asked questions about aliens, they never mentioned the yellow light. I guess they didn't know about it. General Mike and I were always careful not to mention it in reports. They would have to read piles of papers written by other Zoonauts to uncover that secret.

Since it was getting late, they adjourned the meeting. The head Senator said they would return us all to Texas, while the committee made its decisions. Then they left. As we were returning to our cages, an odd thing happened. One young Senator, who had listened more than he had talked, returned to say a few words to Dr. Brooks. They shook hands, the Senator smiled at the rest of us, and left. "Who was that?" I asked.

"That's Senator Al Gore. He has just been elected as Vice President. He agrees to do all he can for us, if we let him use our information about the toy circuits for the benefit of the country."

Kongo groaned. "For the benefit of the military, you mean."

Dr. Wagoner shook his head. "Communications and medical monitoring, tracking hardware and software for ecological uses, and for NASA."

Kongo sighed deeply, as only a large gorilla can sigh, and rubbed the place in his throat that held his 'mike'. "I guess smart bombs and laser weapons could limit the number of civilian casualties, if we ever go to war. Oh well, perhaps the Senator will keep his word."

Apparently he did. For the next eight years, he helped us out more than we ever imagined.

ZONAUTS

Eleven: Animalville USA

Our government can move fast when it wants to. Animalville was all up and in place by the time we got back to Texas from Washington. The location was an abandoned desert amusement park, taken over by lizards and tumbleweeds—40 acres of crumbling buildings and rides, west of Houston. It took a horde of carpenters and painters to clean it up when NASA got it for us in 1992.

I should give you some background on Animalville. The first half of the twentieth century in America, before television, was the golden age for traveling shows. Circuses, Wild West Shows and Carnivals (or carnys) moved by wagons, trucks and trains crisscrossing the nation. In 1955, Disneyland opened, followed by a swarm of large theme parks all over the country. American families were suddenly jumping into their station wagons, hitting brand new interstate highways, driving to these huge parks, to ride roller-coasters, buy souvenirs and eat junk food. Since no one was interested in touring shows any more, they closed. Others, like Texas Bob's Wild West Show, bought land and tried to become mini-parks. Most failed. Texas Bob hung on until the late 1970s, then moved to Florida to sell cars.

The Secret of Animalville

Even after we moved in, the Wild West Show looked like a fallen-down Texas ghost town / closed amusement park. A fifteen-foot wood and plastic statue of Texas Bob still stands at the edge of town, near the old front gate. Wires for telephones, televisions and internet connections run into Bob's head, because that is where Mungo the Parrot decided to make his home. The gorillas, chimpanzees and other primates have redone the Funhouse Spook Ride into a series of pleasant apartments and workshops for their hobbies. The dogs have taken over the Game stalls, and the pond is home to the secretive frogs and toads. The Merry-Go-Round is where we animals meet to discuss our problems. Texas Bob's Yee-Haw Bar-Be-Que is now the library. Luna and the other cats, being cats, stay wherever they want.

I wanted to name the place I.Q. Zoo, but Mungo's research showed that the name was already take by some clowns in Hot Springs, Arkansas. You know, pigs pretending to drive cars and the like. Someday, we plan to go visit them for a hoot. I understand they have a new show, Titanic, starring Leonardo Duck Caprio and Kate Wingslet. "Zoo I.Q." was also out, since the government wanted to keep our true nature hush, hush. Anyway, the name Animalville stuck.

Since the early years, a triple line of fences with warning signs and lights, has sealed the

ZONAUTS

perimeter of Animalville. There is no gate, so to get into Animalville, the Strouds and other human visitors come by helicopter, small plane (there is an airstrip) or through an underground tunnel and parking garage to a secret elevator into the phony Texas Bob's Saloon. Here Tom and Angie Stroud maintain a fully-equipt veterinary hospital, complete with a psychic research unit. There are also living quarters for the Stroud family and guest quarters for other visitors, though that rarely happens. You don't keep a secret by letting people drop in, so usually the only guest is Dr. Brooks Wagoner.

That first night, after we looked over the place, we met in Texas Bob's Saloon to learn the nature of our mission from Dr. Brooks. He said the most important thing of the night.

"The US Government is now convinced that you are too valuable to be harmed or neglected," he said. There was a sigh of relief. No one was going to cut us open to see how we worked. "They are not yet convinced that aliens are involved. That's hard for them to believe—Heck, it's hard for me to believe—but until we know differently, that's the course we're going to take—".

"Keep watching the skies," Mungo croaked harshly. Mungo had just discovered that he could imitate other voices and he was becoming a wealth of old movie lines. Dr. Brooks raised an eyebrow and looked at him, before going on.

"Essentially, yes. We must use all means to determine whether aliens are visiting this planet, whether they have been modifying Zoonauts, and their intentions. Now, as you know, General McIntosh...uh, General Mike, believed they were hostile." I nodded, remembering our conversation.

"But none of us has seen an alien," said Nikki, a golden retriever. "How are we supposed to recognize one if we meet him...her, uh...them?"

"Shoot first and ask questions later," drawled Mungo in his best John Wayne imitation. Kongo glared at him.

"Enough, bird," the big gorilla rumbled. Mungo subsided, watching him. "Nikki has a point. We've never seen an alien, only what aliens do. We are what they do. No human could do this to us. So I believe that we must carefully watch for other signs of alien interference with animals. Eventually they'll become impatient or careless. Like this case in Australia."

"Exactly," said Dr. Brooks. "The Australians have not sent any animals into space, yet a koala bear was found at night in the Alice Springs Public Library reading books. He is very intelligent, and as soon as Dr. Stroud finishes fitting him with a mike we should have an answer to this puzzle."

ZOONAUTS

I shook feathers to get attention. Excuse me Dr. Brooks. First, koalas are marsupials, not bears. Second, with a declining Russian space program, fewer animals go into space. Maybe aliens are coming to earth with their yellow light.Perhaps we will meet them and Mungo added, but Suzy quieted him quickly with a glare. Dr. Brooks went on,

"Since you mention Russians, I will tell you that Russian Zoonauts will join Animalville soon. Please make them welcome and introduce them to our market economy.

It was Kongo's turn to ask something, "And what about our investment plans?"

"Yes, Kongo, you are supposed to continue as before, but you must report all your findings directly to Vice President Gore. That is an important part of this agreement."

After that, events began to move very quickly. We did have a bad moment when the Governor of Texas made a request to visit all NASA installations in Houston, and that included us too. When they told him that we were off limits, he got rather angry about it, but Dr. Brooks was firm and I think the Governor got a call from the White House suggesting that he look elsewhere. At the time, we didn't worry about this much, but it would come back to haunt us eventually.

The Secret of Animalville

Two weeks later the Russians arrived. There were three dogs, fourteen monkeys, two cats and an assortment of frogs and insects. Their leader, Laika, was a Siberian husky named after the first Zoonaut, a female Russian dog who had gone into space in 1957. Laika was old, even by Zoonaut standards, and was very wise. Most of the Russian Zoonauts spoke English and Laika was very fluent. The Russians had been aware of their Zoonauts' special abilities since 1987, but with their shrinking budget for space exploration under the new Russian economy, they had decided to send their Zoonauts to us. The Russian Zoonauts became a welcome addition.

Laika and Kongo seemed drawn to each other, first as fellow leaders, then as thinkers, and finally as friends. They spent much of their time together, talking over the questions of how to learn more about the aliens. I must add something. Although I was the oldest Zoonaut, I never considered myself their leader. I was General Mike's assistant until his death, and then I became our historian, leaving leadership to Kongo. Kongo was certainly our best choice. He works closely with the Strouds, handles all investments and generally watches out for us.

We were just celebrating our eight years in Animalville when things started to get complicated again. The presidential election had just happened, but no one knew then whether Mr. Gore, the Vice President, or Mr. Bush, the Governor of Texas, was going to be President. They were still counting votes in Florida. This bothered Kongo and Laika greatly. If Mr. Bush took over the government, there might be a new attitude about Animalville, especially if the former Governor of Texas remembered how we refused to let him visit Animalville the last time. We still had plenty of money though Kongo had scaled back our toy chip programs. Royalty payments and investments on Abaroatronics games were still arriving every month. We are still safely making some money in bear market mutual funds.

Hopefully, NASA and Dr. Brooks would be left in charge, but we might all have to be more political. Mungo was talking about becoming a 'spin doctor.' If it involves talk, he is the bird for the job. That is partly why the Zoonauts were searching for someone else to help their cause when Jen's friend Sara showed up. She has abilities that no one knew, other than us Zoonauts.

We were still pondering this potential crisis when four days later our latest arrival, an Australian koala , called Coughdrop, got his bandages off. Kongo, Laika and I visited him in the infirmary. He was playing checkers with Cody and Jen.

The Secret of Animalville

Somewhere Jen had found a small Australian bush hat, just Coughdrop's size. He wore it jauntily over one ear. Jen made introductions. Coughdrop looked at us with some curiosity before he spoke.

"G'day. Coo-eee, but you're a strange lot. You mean to tell me you've all been up in space?" We nodded, and Kongo smiled.

"Well, I was younger then, and smaller."

"I should hope so, mate," Coughdrop chuckled. "I don't think any shuttle could get off the ground with a payload your size."

"Actually," I said, "I haven't been out in space. I saw that yellow light while I was very high up in a plane. But I understand that you had the experience on the ground."

"Too right, mate," Coughdrop said, pausing to move one of his checkers. "It happened to me out in the Nevernever."

"Nevernever?"

"I believe he means in the outback," said Laika. "The Great Australian Desert."

"Well, yeah, but not too far out. It was near Cooberpeedee. I was high up a eucalyptus tree, staying away from humans, and generally keeping simple. I've seen those koalas on the telly, advertising Australian tourism and airlines. I don't have to tell you it's not like that. I walked on the ground or climbed trees, drank water, ate eucalyptus leaves, and watched out for dingos and snakes. Boring you might say, but a quiet life has its points. All that is a million years away now.

"One night last summer (winter down in Oz) I was curled up in a treetop, keeping warm, thinking about where to find my next meal. There was a light, I'll tell you, mate, a bright light. It came down through the clouds. Now, humans ride in sky-lights, helicopters and planes, so first I thought it was one of them. Then I got a creepy feeling. Something told me it was alien. It acted funny, jinking around like it was lost or confused. Then a really bright search light came out and swept around until it hit me. My head hurt and I passed out. When I awoke, I wasn't alone.

"I was being carried in a small cage between two strange creatures. Like lizards they were, but big, big as humans, and walking upright. They looked different from each other and talking some ruddy gibberish.

I realized that they were taking me to their ship. There was a bright square, an open door.

They walked me up a ramp; set me on a big metal table. I looked around and saw cages with animals against the walls: a goana, a Joey roo, a parrot. They fussed with an empty cage. I realized then (I'd just gotten a lot smarter, remember) that cage — it was for me!

ZONAUTS

"I studied my cage, a little flat one, like you use to cook lobsters. If I arched my back, I could pop it open. So, I did. When it banged open, the big lizards turned around. They saw me, yelled, but by then I was running for the door, thank you very much. One of them hit the door button, but I got out before it closed: away and into the night. By the time they got it open again, I was gone.

"I was in the dark. Suddenly, I realized how smart I was. I also realized what a fix I was in. First, I wished I could save other animals, not a koala-like thought. If I had tried, they just would have caught me. I wouldn't be here telling you this. Yes, I was in the middle of nowhere, with big lizards looking for me, and I tell you square, I didn't feel like a koala. I was as smart as humans and went off looking for them, reasoning the big lizards wouldn't follow me. Too right. I looked back a few times. The aliens cruised over the desert, hunting for me no doubt. I followed a road to where I knew there was a road depot—you call truck stops—near Cooberpeedee where long-haul trucks fill up. I figured if I could stow away on a big long-haul, it'd take me to a city where I could find some smart humans. I could talk to them to learn what had happened to me. I was beginning to understand things in a new way. Human writing used to be a blur. Now letters were squiggly lines that I could tell apart — a great adventure, frightening but exciting to finally begin reading!

"I managed to climb behind the cab of a big sheep hauler, hid among hoses, and there I slept. When I awoke, we were out in the desert. I could smell sheep and hear their sheep-talk. Twice we stopped. I was getting hungry and thirsty, but stayed hidden. That night we rolled into town, and I got off. I found water, eucalyptus leaves and slept a full day. Then I set out to learning about humans. For two weeks I listened to humans talk and read. Luckily, I came upon an open basement window in a dark building. I crept in looking for food, but found something more useful.

"I was in Alice Springs Public Library, and began reading everything. For two months, I crept in nightly to read: dictionaries and grammar books, then maps, histories, and finally science books. I was half way through Charles Darwin's *ORIGIN OF THE SPECIES* when they caught me. I didn't have much trouble letting humans know that I was smarter than the average koala. Caught reading Darwin gave it away. They drove me to some animal behaviorists in Sydney; in two weeks, here. I guess that makes me the first Australian in Animalville, thank you very much."

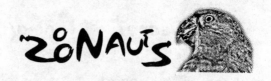

ZONAUTS

Twelve: Methuselah McIntosh, Super Spy

My greatest spy adventure was about to happen! You remember what I told you about Mungo the Parrot. He was fascinated with voices, television, the internet, and anything else involving communication. He was probably the first creature to learn of the tragic events of 911. He lived in the great plastic and wood head of the Texas Bob statue, where he surrounded himself with televisions and computer screens, keyboards, radios, phones and all manner of electronic gear. Sometimes, I worried that all this electricity was frying his little birdy brain. Three times a week—on orders of Dr. Angie Stroud—Mungo had to spend an hour exercising his wings. Flying, around Animalville, which I did with him, partly to make sure that he did it, and partly because I liked him.

Well, on a fine spring day, in 2002, after we had made two circuits of the park and were resting on the old water tower, he said something that I thought was very strange. He said he had picked up a report on Radio India, in Hindi, about two panda bears that had come out of the Himalayan foothills and were living at a monastery, where the monks often consulted them for their wisdom.

The Secret of Animalville

Mungo asked me if I thought that it was a hoax—something dreamed up by a human to get attention—or whether these could be more animals the aliens had changed. I said, "I don't know—I never heard of pandas going into space—but let's call the Indian government and ask them to ship the pandas to us."

Mungo said knowingly, "These pandas aren't in India. They're in Tibet. The Indians heard of the pandas, but no one has seen them."

I thought about it for a moment. Then I told Mungo, "We should go report this to Dr. Tom."

Dr. Tom called Dr. Brooks in Washington D.C. After a few days, we got the information we were waiting for; the pandas were in a monastery near the town of Rima. So far, the Chinese government (which governs Tibet) had not done anything about it. "Maybe they don't believe it," said Mungo. "Yet," he added.

"Well, when the Chinese government finds out perhaps they'll send us pandas," I said. "The Australians sent us Coughdrop." Mungo laughed.

"The Australians have been our friends for many years," he said. "The Chinese government is suspicious of the American government. They won't send the pandas here."

I thought about this. The Chinese had fought us in Korea. They still had a Communist government. This was all human politics, something I had never fully understood, but I did know one thing; an alien invasion was much more important. "Then we must go get them," I said.

They looked at me strangely. I knew, once again, I said something aloud that I should have kept to myself. That is how I wound up on a plane to India with Mungo, Laika and Dr. Tom. We flew to Hawaii, then Australia, then India and now to the Indian Air Force Base at Sadiya.

It was strange going back to India and the Himalayas again, since I had not been there since World War II. As I looked out the window of our special US Air Force jet, I could see the Himalayas shining in the sun. Mount Everest was a hundred miles away but still looked gigantic. Mungo and Laika were dozing so I had a chance to talk to Dr. Tom. "I understand why Kongo couldn't come," I said, "as there are no gorillas in India, and I know we need Mungo because he talks all Chinese dialects, but why Laika?"

"Laika is very wise. Laika also understands some Chinese," Dr. Tom said. "And he's a dog. Dogs are everywhere. No one will notice him."

"Mungo and I are African parrots," I said. "Won't someone notice us?"

"Most people will just see two birds. Only a bird watcher would know the difference. Hopefully you won't be in Tibet long enough to be discovered."

"Ummm." I mulled that over in my head for a bit, then asked the question that had really been bothering me. "And me? Why me?"

"Mungo is smart but he is not wise. He also talks too much. Laika is wise, but he is a dog. As I said, dogs are common and the monks at the monastery may not respect him. You have both wisdom and age. You will speak for Animalville. You are our best spokesman. Spokes-being," he corrected himself. "But there is one other thing."

"Yes?"

"This is likely to be dangerous. If you can't get the pandas out safely, don't risk being hurt or captured. You must make that decision. If it looks too dangerous, then the three of you must get away and back to the border. Don't get lost or wander across the border into Burma. That country isn't any safer for Americans than Tibet."

"I'll bring them home," I said, hoping I was up to it. Just then Laika joined us.

"I heard a thud in the baggage area. I'm going back there to investigate."

"All right Laika, be careful," said Dr. Tom.

I decided to go as backup. Laika and I soon made a startling discovery. We had a young stowaway, Cody.

ZONAUTS

"Excuse me young man, what exactly do you think you're doing here," I interrogated.

"Please don't turn me in," Cody pleaded. "I just had to come along! I can be very useful."

"No you won't!" Laika growled. "You can stay right here in the plane until we fly home."

Cody was clearly intimidated, but I just knew he would get into even more trouble if we didn't supervise him, so I quickly devised a plan.

"Laika," I improvised, "I'm sure Cody can be useful in this mission. Let's keep his presence here a secret between us." Laika wasn't sure, but finally agreed.

At the airport there was a truck waiting. Mungo, Laika and I got in the back while Dr. Tom rode up front with the driver, a Gurkha soldier, who took us to a point where Dr. Tom could study the border. Cody was hiding in our supply bag.

Because the governments of India and China disagreed about where the actual borders should be, each wanting more of the other's territory, the border was fenced. There were watchtowers too. The road from Sadiya to Rima passed through a checkpoint where armed Chinese guards inspected anyone coming from India and armed Indian troops did the same for anyone from China, not that there was much traffic.

Mostly the guards stood around and glared at each other.

"Well," said Mungo. "Methuselah and I can fly over a fence but what about Laika? He can't."

Tom had considered this. "You must fly east along the fence and Methuselah must fly west. When you find a break where Laika may get safely through, return. We'll use the closest one."

As it happened, I found a place where the wire did not completely cover a ravine only 300 yards west of us. At dusk, Mungo and I flew across the border to a rock formation that looked like a crouching bear and waited. Laika crept through under a wire to join us an hour later, dragging the provisions bag, secretly containing Cody. We slept there until dawn.

When the sun was up, we made our way along the road to Rima. At last, we saw the town to the right, and to the left, up the hillside, a tall stone monastery where the monks were holding the pandas. It was a short trip to the monastery, but first I decided that Mungo and I should scout out the town to work out a plan.

There was a busy market in Rima, and there were pilgrims coming through to visit the monastery. There were also Chinese flags and soldiers, but they didn't seem to be particularly excited about anything. All in all, it was a case of humans going about their business, and that was fine for us. We flew back to the hiding spot.

"Cody," I said, "use the supply bag to make a crude tunic and roll around in the dirt a little."

"Cool! ... But why?"

"You and Laika are going to become Buddhist pilgrims, are you ready?"

"Sure, what do I have to do?"

"Join some group entering the monastery."

The Secret of Animalville

Our luck was holding. A group of pilgrims had just arrived at the monastery. They were busy spinning their prayer wheels by the wall. Cody had just enough time to put together his poor robes. He was quite funny to look at.

"You had better let me do the talking," said Laika. "You don't know any Chinese."

"And you don't think they'll notice a talking dog?" Cody retorted.

"Don't argue with me. If it were my decision you'd still be hiding in the plane."

"All right, but once we're inside, follow me. After all, you are 'just' a dog."

The pilgrims were too busy with meditations to notice the young boy and his dog join them. Then a monk unlocked the door and let them all in. Mungo and I saw Laika and Cody slip in with the group. We flew over the wall to meet them. We started searching for the pandas together, but somehow we lost Cody in the crowd of pilgrims. We eventually found the pandas in a main hall and crept in to listen.

The pandas sat on cushions, surrounded by a small circle of monks who listened as the head monk asked the two pandas questions. This leader wore a banana-shaped thing on his head— really an indication of rank, like a bishop's mitre.

ZONAUTS

I could not follow much of it but Mungo translated, interspersed with comments of his own such as "Good answer" and "Well said" and "They are very wise." The discussion seemed to be about the place of humans and animals in the world. The pandas thought out what they would say before each answer and were always polite and courteous. They could not exactly 'speak' but had learned a form of sign language and grunts that the head monk seemed to understand. When they weren't 'speaking,' they lay back on pillows and munched green bamboo shoots. I was just thinking about how to approach the pandas, when a young monk spotted us. He came toward us, waving a broom, to shoo us away, when Laika said, in Chinese, "*Ni dui ke ren shi fen bu li mao* (Are you so impolite to all of your guests?)"

The monk screamed and ran toward the other monks, yelling in Chinese. Chaos followed.

"What is he saying?" I asked Mungo in a hushed whisper.

"*Dong wu hui shuo hua la!*"

The Secret of Animalville

"I mean, what does it MEAN in 'English'?"

"'More talking animals!' that's all."

The attention of the monks and the pandas suddenly turned on us. I could only think of one thing to say. "Follow me." I hopped to the floor and walked forward, Laika following behind with Mungo perched on his back. I tried to look impressive, but parrots are not designed to look regal while walking, so I nodded and just kept saying "*ne hao* (hello)" in Chinese. The monks backed away to give us a clear path.

Finally, we stood face to face with the two pandas. The head monk with the banana head-piece was attending them. We all bowed. "Greetings," I said. "I am Methuselah. I am here as a representative of Animalville, where the talking animals have gathered." I waited for Mungo to catch up with translating it into Tibetan and Chinese, "*Ne hao, wo shu Methuselah. Wo shu dong wu dai biao.*"

The first question was easy, "*Ni chi fan la ma*? (Have you eaten yet?)", a typical Chinese greeting, requiring Mungo's polite response, "*Chi la. Ni na*? (Yes I have eaten. Have you?).

Tom had said to keep it simple, but the head monk's next question was a problem.

"*Ni lai zi shang tian ma*? (Are you from the gods of the sky?)"

ZONAUTS

Tom and I had talked about lying. I hate to lie, but Dr. Tom said that the most important thing was to protect Animalville. If I had to make something up to do that, well, that's what spies do. Up until that moment, I had not thought of myself as a spy. I knew about spies. I also knew that captured spies were usually shot. I carefully pondered the monk's question before answering.

"The sky beings give us our powers, yes." Which was true. The monks suddenly began to talk excitedly among themselves until the head monk pounded his stick on the floor.

"Are the pandas your brothers and sisters?"

"Yes. All animals are brothers under the sky." There was more excited talking. In the commotion, I noticed one of the pandas signing something to Mungo. "What is he saying?"

"He says, 'You're doing fine. Keep it mystical. They like that.'" So, I did. I told how many animals had received mystical powers and how we were charged with the responsibility of saving Earth, how the animals had gathered in a secret town, and that we needed the pandas to come with us since their wisdom would be much appreciated. The monks listened carefully. While they clearly were in awe of us, it was also obvious that they didn't want to give up their pandas. The old monk looked unhappy.

The Secret of Animalville

As they talked, I learned more through Mungo's translations. The pandas were called Hsing-Hsing and Ling-Ling and they were a mated pair, which meant that they had been living as a couple in the forest until the night the bright yellow light hit them. They awakened before the aliens could capture them, and fled westward until they came to this monastery. The monks were very good to them, but the head monk did not want them to leave. They were virtual prisoners until we arrived. Now there was a good chance the monks would keep us too.

"I wonder about that," said Laika, who was watching two monks closing grills over the windows, perhaps so we couldn't fly out. I thought they would consider us spies, not captives. At that moment, I figured that my long strange career was about to end, when another monk ran in toward us. To our amazement, it was Cody! He had traded in his ragged sack tunic for a monastic robe. He was clearly a master of disguise.

"Quick, we must do something!" Cody whispered to Laika. "Some army trucks are heading this way. I just spotted them from the top of the roof."

We didn't have time to ask him what he had been doing there or how he got his new clothes.

"What, please, did this novice just tell you?" asked Hsing-Hsing.

"He has seen a great vision that you must leave with us immediately," said Laika.

Pointing to the windows, Cody shouted out, "*Kuai lai kan*! (Look!)," in flawless Chinese.

Everyone ran to the windows. I flew over and perched where I could see out. Three large green trucks were coming up the road to the monastery. The monks all started shouting.

"Chinese soldiers," yelled Mungo over the din, "coming to take the pandas away." But the head monk had pulled back a curtain, revealing a dark opening, and he was motioning us toward it. Hsing-Hsing, Ling-Ling, Cody and Laika ran toward it, Mungo and I flying overhead. As we reached the exit, we heard a distant pounding. Chinese soldiers were breaking down the door.

The head monk turned to us then, and said in almost perfect English, "You must go, and take the pandas with you. We shall miss them, but it would be worse if the Chinese captured them."

"You speak English?"

"Yes," said the monk. "I worked with the American Air Force during the war."

"So did I," I said, and added, "Thank you, very much," and bowed, then hurried after Ling-Ling into the opening, which turned out to be a stairway that went down, a very long way.

The stairway led us to a cave, where we waited until the sun went down over the Himalayas. Then, with Laika leading, Mungo and I each riding a panda, we made our way back to the ravine where Laika had come under the wire. That was when I realized what I hadn't taken into account.

The opening that was big enough for Laika and Cody to slip under was much too small for the pandas. It was a bad moment, and we all looked at each other, until Laika spoke up.

"Well, I'm still a dog." Laika began to dig, to enlarge the hole under the wire. As he did so the pandas, although not well suited for moving earth, pushed away the dirt that Laika had dug out, so it wouldn't clog up the hole. Mungo and I perched where we could watch out for trouble. It wasn't long before we found it.

First we saw the lights of vehicles coming down toward the border, then the blowing of whistles and shouted orders in Chinese. "They're coming to search the fence for the pandas," Mungo said. "We must do something."

"In case you noticed, I'm not James Bond," I said crossly.

"No, but you read everything. Do Chinese believe in ghosts?"

"Yes! Yes they do."

"Good," said Mungo. "Here's the plan..."

As the Chinese soldiers came down the fence toward us, their officer suddenly began screaming at them, calling them back, telling them to return to the trucks. This, of course, was Mungo, who had flown down to the border crossing and listened to the officer long enough to learn how he spoke. It wasn't hard for Mungo, who is a perfect mimic. After some confusion, the Chinese soldiers turned around and left. However, it wasn't long before they returned.

This time their officer was with them, driving them forward with curses and threats, but Mungo and I were ready. Hiding in the darkness we began making eerie sounds. I had no idea what

Chinese ghosts were supposed to sound like, but I figured 'woo-ooohhh' would probably work. It did. The soldiers stopped and began chattering wildly.

"*Zhan zhu! Gan sha de?* (Stop! What are you doing here?)", Mungo wailed in Chinese. The Chinese soldiers were all talking at once, their officer trying to yell above the racket. "They say I am a ghost of the mountain," Mungo said proudly.

"Well, don't disappoint them," I said. "Give them a story to take home."

Mungo puffed himself up and bellowed, "*Wo shi shan yao. Gun Kai! King! Kong! King! Kong! King! Kong! ...* (I am the Ghost of the Mountain. Leave this place! Now!)" We all rattled the metal fence while he added a torrent of Chinese words. With screams, the Chinese soldiers broke and fled, their officer firing in the air to stop them. They ignored him and soon disappeared into the darkness.

Not wishing to see if they would come back again, Mungo and I hurried to the wire where Hsing-Hsing was just squeezing through. Ling-Ling, Laika and Cody were on the other side.

"I heard shooting," said Laika. "Was there trouble?"

"Oh no," chirped Mungo. "It was fun."

For once I had to agree with him. I turned to Cody, "Where did you learn Chinese?"

ZONAUTS

"Oh, I've been taking lessons from Mungo."
"I should have guessed!" I replied.

Three hours later we were all aboard the US Air Force jet, heading for home. On the way, Laika the dog tried to teach the Panda's to say 'Hello, President Bush', but they were very confused. It sounded to them as if Laika was saying, *"Hei gou, pian za-da, bu shi?"* the way Japanese soldiers try to speak in Chinese. Laika kept trying to tell them it was polite, but they refused to believe him or repeat it to him. We all roared with laughter when they confessed that the meaning of the sound is 'Are you a cheating dog?' They would never say that to Laika!

The Secret of Animalville

Thirteen: Aliens Revealed

When we got back, the team felt like celebrities. Laika accompanied Hsing-Hsing and Ling-Ling to meet our new President, Mr. Bush.

I was ready for a good hot bath, and a long nap! After resting up for a few days, I went to see Mungo in his command center, Texas Bob's head. As usual, he was typing away on a keyboard while watching three video screens.

"You'll go blind one of these days, you know that?" I said. Mungo just laughed.

"I've been telling him that but he won't believe me," drawled Luna, a long lean gray cat that had come to us with Laika and the other Russians. Luna was fascinated with Mungo. She was trying to understand his obsession with technology, and liked to tease him about it. When I asked Mungo if this bothered him he said, "Bothered? By Luna? No, she's my biggest fan. Someday, when I'm running the Tonight Show, I'll make her my announcer."

Luna curled up on a large speaker, watching Mungo surf the net. She favored me with a disturbing cat smile (I am a bird, after all) and ghosted away. That's Luna's power. She can 'ghost' through solid objects, walls and such. Not even a smile remains. I shook my head.

"Silly cat. ... Mungo, you called me?"

"Yes. On the news, this morning, there was a story out of China. The Chinese government is blaming India for the theft of the two pandas. The Indian government has no idea what they're talking about."

"Oh dear, hope we didn't start a war," I said.

"I don't think so," Mungo laughed. "The head monk at the monastery gave an interview to a French reporter. He said the pandas weren't pandas at all but space creatures, and they've gone back to space. After that, the Chinese are going to look pretty silly if they keep this up."

"That's why I came to see you," I said. "Hsing-Hsing and Ling-Ling have started talking. I thought you'd like to be there."

We flew to Texas Bob's Ye-Haw Bar-Be-Que, where many animals had gathered with the Strouds and Dr. Brooks. We first found a perch in the rafters near the owls, Horace and Plato, but then I decided to join Jen and Cody. Hsing-Hsing and Ling-Ling were sitting between the Strouds. Their throats were unbandaged. I found out later that Dr. Tom only went in through their mouths to implant the Mikes. To ease their throats, still sore from the operation, each panda had a tall glass of lemonade. As Mungo and I flew in, Kongo was just rising to his feet.

He leaned forward on his knuckles, cleared his throat, a sound Mungo insisted was like an avalanche. He called us to order. "My friends, we have great and grave news. We now know where the aliens come from and what they want."

There was a sudden blast of sound as everyone began talking, but Kongo raised a huge hand and the noise subsided again. Besides being our leader and respected by all of us, he also happens to be a large and powerful gorilla.

"The same yellow light that we saw has changed our two newest members, Hsing-Hsing and Ling-Ling while in a bamboo forest of southern China. While no one yet knew what Ling-Ling's power was, Hsing-Hsing's power was both important and amazing. He will tell us more."

Now, I've mentioned some super animal powers, like the ability to fly or turn invisible. Other powers affect objects, allowing an animal to move or bend objects, or, like Luna, to ghost through walls. Some involve mental feats, such as Mungo's ability with language or my memory. Others involve perception. Nikki the Dog hears at great distances. A few involve altering reality, such as when Laika projects a defensive shield or Kongo briefly stops time. But Hsing-Hsing's power brought us the most direct knowledge of the aliens themselves.

Hsing-Hsing took a sip of lemonade and looked out at us. When he spoke, his accent was still heavily Chinese, but I could tell he was learning English fast, perhaps as fast as Mungo.

"My friends. First, I must greet you for to bring my mate Ling-Ling and me to you fine country. The last few weeks are very...confused for us. So much...many new things sit in our heads, that it is almost not possible to speak of them. A new land, a new speaking of language..." Here, Ling-Ling leaned in close to Hsing-Hsing and whispered something. He smiled.

"A new...learning a new language, yes. And thing which you call a power." He looked at Tom Stroud, who nodded. "I will let Dr. Thomas Stroud tell you of it. His words better than me."

Dr. Tom stood up and every furry, feathered or scaled head in the place focused on him. "We know that when Hsing-Hsing and Ling-Ling came to in the forest after seeing the yellow light, they were alone. There were no aliens there, and they had the presence of mind to immediately leave the area. They traveled west for weeks, ending up at the Rima monastery, where Mungo, Methuselah and Laika found them and helped them escape."

At this, Hsing-Hsing nodded to me with a smile. Again, I felt immensely proud sitting on Cody's shoulder. Cody tapped me on a wing. "How about that? You're a hero now," Cody said with a wink. "I never get to do anything, sigh."

"Don't start!" I whispered, "You're just lucky I didn't tell anyone about your prank young man."

"Shhhh", said Jen from nearby.

Dr. Tom went on. "We believe that this time the aliens actually touched the pandas, because of the power they have. Why the aliens left without them, well, perhaps the pandas were too large, or the aliens learned something that scared them. At any rate, before the aliens left, Hsing-Hsing absorbed their memories. We now know who the aliens are, where they come from, and what they want."

The hall was so quiet you could hear a pin drop. "Their dark planet swings in an astrosynchronous orbit behind Alpha Centauri."

"...which means it is not visible from Earth, though human astronomers have long suspected its presence", Cody whispered in my ear, a fact he may have picked up in science class, but more likely from Kongo.

"Amador is rich in minerals, poor in everything else, including breathable air and drinkable water. The best parts look like a slum in Hell.

ZONAUTS

Volcanoes, fire pits, fumaroles, lava flows, and other charming features pit the landscape. Great factories turn out large menacing machines. Occasionally a mountain blows up or island sinks into the alkaline seas. The worst about the place are the Amadorians themselves, who may have conquered the universe long ago if they were more numerous. They have a low birth rate."

Cody couldn't resist another comment. "Would you like to be born on Amador?" I said nothing; Jen just stared at him with beady eyes.

"At present, there are only a few thousand of them. The average Amadorian is awesomely creepy, and you have seen them before."

This last point attracted Kongo's attention, "What do you mean, we have seen them before, where?"

"Amadorians come in all shapes and sizes. No two are alike. They look like every possible variety and design of what we on Earth call a 'dragon', those creatures of myth and legend that never really existed. Or did they?"

"Do they really exist," asked Jen, and if so how did they get here so long ago?"

"At least a thousand years ago, a group of thirty or forty Amadorians who decided to stop fighting each other and cooperate, built a junky spaceship. They reached Earth, where they began terrorizing the human population; burning forests, eating maidens, and squabbling over loot. They were most happy in China, where the people worshiped them as rain gods. It was their squabbling that did them in, along with an embarrassing development. Armored humans called knights, riding armored horses, kept sticking them with lances. After a particularly famous knight named George killed Ospumunt, the Amadorian leader, the surviving Amadorians gave up and fled home. A few kept visiting China, since every twelve years they honored dragons."

"During their rather brief stay, Amadorians noticed something about Earth. Everything bred like crazy here; high birth rates. If the Amadorians could settle on Earth, they might increase their numbers. Galactic domination might then become possible. So they watched Earth and waited. They weren't happy with what they saw."

"Humans have a genius for war, and a succession of human inventions (gunpowder, steamships, aircraft, atomic bombs) depressed the Amadorians to the point that they almost gave up ...almost that is. Then, humans started carrying animals into orbit and Amadorians saw their chance. If they could change and mutate these animals to make them superior, they might be able to recruit them as mercenaries in a war against the humans for possession of Earth. Then

ZONAUTS

a few Amadorians might command millions of animals and wipe the humans out. They just wouldn't tell their brave animal soldiers that they planned to eat them later. So, they positioned satellites with mutagenic rays in the Asteroid belt, and waited. But the rays could not penetrate the Earth's atmosphere, so only animals in space or very high up in airplanes were affected at first."

"When the animals were changed, the Amadorians got another disappointment. Very few of the intelligent animals were eager to make war on humans, for war is not usually an intelligent business."

"There are a few Amadorians you should all know about, it is in the briefing that Laika is passing out now. With an army like this, only draconian discipline assures that they get anything done. Their own meanness is their Achilles' heel."

BRIEFING ON KNOWN AMADORIANS

ARA-GATAN. The scheming Leader of the Amadorians looks like an immensely old and spiny winged dragon. His palace is filled with maps, planetary models, files, plots, plans, intelligence estimates and Toadies—creepy Amadorians, willing to serve his every whim. There aren't many jobs on Amador, and Palace Toady is a good job.

Ara-Gatan wants desperately to conquer the universe, but he's old, and he'll settle for conquering

The Secret of Animalville

ANYTHING at this point. Since Earth is the closest livable planet and the best possibility, Ara-Gatan is putting all of his energy into the project. He's a blustery old scab, more of a Mussolini than a Hitler. He likes to pose and plot.

TRE-POK. He is General MacArthur on a bad day; Patton with a thorn in his paw. This Warlord is the head of the Amadorian armed forces and he is BIG TROUBLE. He envies anything he hasn't conquered, and despises anything he has. He is determined to rub out Earth and he'll sweep aside anyone or anything that stands in his way—including Ara-Gatan, if it comes to that. In fact, there is only one thing that he fears...

THE HIGH ROTOCASTER. This tall, spindly, ethereal Dragon is the sage and mystic, spiritual advisor and Grand Poobah of the Amadorian Power Structure. He's also the only Amadorian who still follows the old ways—what humans might call magic, or ESP. He can disappear disobedient subordinates (which is what happened to Tre-Pok's predecessor) but he generally moves through life in his own private fog. He is loyal to Ara-Gatan, but otherwise even more unpredictable than the average Amadorian.

AMADORIAN ARMED FORCES. They fight with energy weapons and armored vehicles, or with bare claws and teeth—if there's anyone to fight. Being generally stuck on Amador, where life is hard enough, they are not allowed to kill each other because of the low birth rate. In space, they travel in banged battle cruisers and transports that look like

ZONAUTS

they were designed by a junkyard dog. On the efficiency side, they get Amadorians to where they're going, and the weapons are deadly. On the inefficiency side, the average Amadorian warrior has his own agenda involving feeding, looting and blowing things up, so they have to be commanded with an iron hand and are usually sent out in twos to keep an eye on each other. Typical of these warrior teams are...

FISHWICK AND KORNBLEND. These relatively young Amadorian males (150 years old) are Scout pilots, which means that they make a lot of flights to Earth, to repair spy satellites, interfere with NASA launches, make crop circles, mutilate cows, and generally be a nuisance. Fishwick considers himself a philosopher, which in his case means that he loves to quote trite sayings from the The Amadorian Codex and spout pompous slogans. This drives his co-pilot crazy and the proscription against killing fellow Amadorians is probably the only reason Fishwick hasn't been sent floating into orbit without a breather suit.

Kornblend is Fishwick's opposite, the Amadorian dragon of action, a cold-blooded would-be killer who secretly watches Clint Eastwood and Bruce Willis movies from earth satellite broadcasts. Stallone and Schwartzenegger drive him into a frenzy. Kornblend secretly admires and fears Earthlings, thinking that most of them go through life blowing things up, running cars off cliffs, and shooting each other. "How can we conquer such a people?" he is fond of asking. "Through Ultimate Violence!"

Fourteen: Little Knowledge

After the briefing, it all fit into place. We were fascinated by what we just learned from Hsing-Hsing about these aliens, but all confessed that we didn't know what more we could do as a result.

They were out there, in a place where they could not be seen. They came here when they wished, and apparently we couldn't see their ships either, at least on radar, and when we got close enough to see them with the naked eye, we were begging to be shot. Then Mungo came up with an interesting idea.

"If we could see their ships, who do you think would be seeing them?"

"Well," I said, scratching my feathers with a claw. "All sorts of people."

"And what do they call people who see flying saucers?"

"Well, they usually call them crazy. But, what about the Air Force? They must see them all the time." And I knew. "National Security. They wouldn't tell anyone."

"Right," said Mungo. "The Air Force could be at war with the Amadorians and not tell us. So, how do we tell the Air Force what we now know?"

ZONAUTS

"We don't,' I said. Then I told him about Mr. Valentine and Mr. Christmas and the visit from the National Security Agency. Mungo was so angry that he hopped from one foot to the other and said words I hoped he didn't use around Jen and Cody.

"But that's insane. Do you mean to say that there's an agency of the government whose job it is to keep people from talking to each other?"

"More than one, I'd guess. They're very worried about secrets getting out." I told him about spies, counterspies, codes, decoders, and for once Mungo sat quietly and listened, his full attention on me. Then I told him about the National Security Agency (NSA), the Central Intelligence Agency (CIA), the Defense Intelligence Agency (DIA), the Federal Bureau of Investigation (FBI) and the Secret Service.

"But, with so many different spy agencies, how do they get anything done?"

I laughed. "A lot of people ask that question. Now the President wants to start a new one, Homeland Security. I'm going to talk to Dr. Tom," I said. "Maybe he and Dr. Brooks know what to do." Mungo just looked at me. "What?" I said. "What are you thinking?"

"Ohhhh...nothing. But I'll let you know if I come up with any ideas." And he flew off. I should have followed him. I should have known that he'd get into trouble, but I was already deep in thought about Jen's friend Sarafina Flores-Abaroa. We had met a couple of times when Jen was over at her house. It was really her grandmother's house, since she was nearly orphaned, after her father died and mother ran away to Utah. That is when I got the idea that special children, children like Sara, were important for our battle with Amador, not the government.

Mungo started disappearing for days at a time. I covered for him for as much as I could, but when he started missing his mandatory exercise flights too, I decided it was time to investigate. Of course, I found him in his command center in Texas Bob's plastic head.

Mungo and Horace the Owl were sitting before one of the monitors, looking at what appeared to me to be alphabet soup, random numbers and letters scrolling across the screen. Then Miss Baker the Squirrel Monkey popped out from behind one of Mungo's computers, a wire in one hand and a soldering gun in the other.

"Hello, Methuselah." she said brightly. "Come to help us with the project?"

Mungo and Horace turned suddenly, staring at me, both of them appearing horribly guilty. "Ix-nay on the oject-pray," Mungo whispered.

ZONAUTS

"What project?" I said warily. "What have you been up to?"

"Well…" said Mungo.

"Well…" said Horace.

Well, I had had enough! I had a sinking feeling that I knew what they were doing, and just how much trouble we were all in. "I think we had best go talk to Dr. Tom," I said.

Dr. Tom took it better than I did. He stayed calm. I wanted to pluck out all of Mungo's feathers and drop him from a great height, but Tom merely sat and listened until the three culprits were finished talking.

"Let me get this straight," he said. "You've been trying to break Air Force's codes so you can get a look at whatever they know about aliens?"

"Oh no," Mungo said. "We broke their codes last week. We're trying to break into—" Horace let out a shrill screech, and fixed his stern eyes on Mungo.

"Are you sure you want to get into this?" he said.

"Get into what?" Dr. Tom and I said together. I shook my head, but Dr. Tom kept his cool. He also knew just how to get results.

"Mungo, if you don't tell me everything, I'm going to cut all wires that lead into your quarters."

The Secret of Animalville

Mungo let out a shriek, then hung his head. "I'm sorry. Okay, Dr. Tom, I'll tell you everything." He did. It seems that breaking Air Force's codes weren't enough for them. After finding out what the Air Force knew about Amador, Mungo decided to find out who else knew, so they broke into the NSA databank in Greenbriar, West Virginia.

"That must be the most secure computer in the world. I'm surprised we don't have NSA agents swarming all over Animalville now," Dr. Tom said. "You know they back-trace a break-in."

"We were very careful," Horace confided.

"I hope so," said Dr. Tom, "but shut down the code-breaking operation, now." Mungo, Horace and Miss Baker promised they would. I also hoped that we were not too late.

When we saw Air Force data on Amador, I almost decided Mungo's little escapade was worth it. The Air Force had been tangling with Amadorian spacecraft for years. There were dozens of pictures of what the Air Force decided were scout ships. Oddly, they all looked homemade, like someone had built them in a garage from junkyard parts. They were mostly football-shaped. Each was about fifty feet long, but no two looked alike. They had guns, rocket tubes and windows oddly placed. Some had designs painted on them. I was familiar with our Air Force, having served with

ZONAUTS

General Mike. Each plane, helicopter and missile looked the same; built in factories, on assembly lines, with identical parts. These Amadorian ships made no sense. I questioned Hsing-Hsing, whose English was then much improved.

"Well," said Hsing-Hsing, as Ling-Ling prepared a snack for us of tasty bamboo shoots, "first you must remember that there aren't many of them, only a few thousand. Which means they can't do things the way we do on earth. There are factories on earth where over 5,000 humans work, more than all Amadorians. I think each Amadorian has to build his own ship."

"That would explain these pictures."

"Yes," said Hsing-Hsing. "Their ships are customized, like hot-rods. But hot-rods start out as identical cars. I think that these ships did too."

I puzzled, "Start as cars? I don't get it."

Hsing-Hsing laughed his merry panda laugh. Ling-Ling smiled. They were very much in love. "No, but that's the right idea. Notice, these ships are all about the same size and shape. They probably had a lot of old ships sitting around; perhaps thousands. Perhaps ships were left over from a war; what humans call 'surplus.' This suggests there were once more Amadorians."

I nodded. "So, we have a few thousand Amadorians in a few thousand very old spaceships trying to conquer a planet with five billion people and trillions of animals. They've been trying for how long?"

Hsing-Hsing spread his paws and shrugged. "At least since World War Two, possibly longer, if you count the forty or so who came to earth a thousand years ago, and ruled China for a while."

"This doesn't sound like a serious threat," I said. Hsing-Hsing munched on a bamboo shoot for a long time before answering.

"But they did take over China for a while. Now they have a few thousand working spaceships with guns. Rockets, they can get here. The last time I checked, we had a couple of shuttles and one space station. They are picking off those one at a time. Targeting us is easy for them since we have no guns up there; no rockets; no phasers, masers, lasers, photon torpedoes or defensive shields. Get my point?"

I fixed him with my best General Mike flint-and-steel stare. "We have us," I said. "I think it's time we did something about it. We have got to get people to listen. The children are the key and Sara will let us know how. I just know that. It's time to talk with Jen about all of this."

Zonauts

Fifteen: Complications

We were hoping to hear nothing more about Mungo's break into the NSA database at Greenbriar, West Virginia, but I guess that no one is that lucky. Less than a week later, Mungo and Horace detected and foiled no fewer than nineteen attempts to hack into our computer systems. After this, the hackers stopped a while. Mungo was very chuffed up about our security and his ability to make our systems hacker-proof, until Kongo pointed out that we wouldn't be having these problems if he hadn't hacked into Greenbriar in the first place. It was risking our financial deals, which especially angered Kongo.

Next, Mungo picked up re-targeting instructions to a spy satellite. We all stayed undercover for ten days as Animalville was photographed from orbit, meaning spies knew our location. Most animals were angry about that.

Then we had problems with aircraft and helicopters nosing around. Dr. Tom called Dr. Brooks, who called an officer at the Johnson Space Center. That officer put through a call to a special Air Force unit at William Hobby Field. Suddenly the sky was full of jets and we had no more trouble with people trying to fly over Animalville, until Columbia exploded over us.

Cars began stopping on Interstate 90 and people began taking pictures of Animalville with telephoto lenses, so Laika sent Horace and Plato the owls out to get their license numbers. Mungo ran them through the computer. Most of them turned out to be registered to various government agencies—CIA, DIA, FBI—or not registered at all, so we kept everyone away from that side of Animalville. Dr. Brooks made some calls in Washington. Those cars stopped visiting.

Some attempts to find out about us were almost funny. Two FBI agents named Musgrave and Skelton managed to replace two men who drive the truck that picks up our garbage each week. They got as far as our underground parking garage where they found a squad of Air Force security troops waiting for them. They were returned to the FBI with a warning.

Then a woman named Susan LaBlanc, who turned out to be a reporter for a newspaper called *The National Revealer*, started following Jen and Cody home from school. When the Air Force driver realized that they were being followed, he radioed the Harris County Sheriff who pulled the woman over and gave her car a safety inspection. After three days of this, and fix-it tickets totaling $790, she gave up.

ZONAUTS

A note about the Air Force: on the one hand they were carrying on a private 'almost-war' with Amadorians and not telling us. On the other hand, the Air Force was responsible for our safety and security. They usually did a good job. If that sounds confusing, it's because the Air Force and the government are very large, and just because you were a member of an organization didn't mean they tell you anything. Dr. Brooks once told me that only fourteen people outside of Animalville knew about us, including the President and Vice President. We tried to keep it that way. Then an old problem reappeared.

One February night, early in 2003, after things had just calmed down from the Columbia disaster, Nikki was out for a walk. Nikki's ability is greatly increased hearing, so she usually slept during the day to avoid all noise. She spent nights patrolling Animalville.

Shortly after Jen's school report that led to Sara learning about Animalville, events got even stranger. Early one morning, while walking past the Saloon, Nikki heard a break in. She stopped, listened again, and went to find Dr. Tom. She couldn't locate him, so she woke up Cody.

"What is it, Nikki? It's too early for games."

The Secret of Animalville

"Someone is breaking into Animalville. I can hear them."

"Are you sure? There are three fences out there, all of them electrified, with cameras too." This is true, but we had made a mistake. Our cameras were not watched by people or animals, but by a computer. Computers can be fooled, as Mungo often informs us.

"Why didn't you bother my dad?" Cody asked, finally realizing it was something serious.

"I wanted to, but I can't find him anywhere."

"That's because he's away on some special investigation." The two pivoted around to see Jen standing at the doorway; ready for action.

"This is probably your fault for telling Sara everything the other day," Cody accused.

"That was Methuselah's fault, not mine!"

"Well, anyway its up to us now to check this out," said Cody, pulling on his shoes.

"Should I wake mom or the others?"

"Not yet," said Jen. "I'll take a radio. If there's trouble we can call." The three went off to find the fence break, which turned out to be at the far northeast corner of Animalville.

"Why didn't our alarm buzz?" Cody puzzled.

"Elementary my dear Cody," Nikki replied, "Someone has cut the fence and used wires with alligator clips to carry electricity around the break..."

"...without setting off alarms!" Jen finished, "but who?"

Cody shined his flashlight at a camera that covered this section and found a wire leading from it to a portable VCR.

"What is that?" asked Jen.

"The more important question is 'What is it doing?' Look closely!" Nikki advised. She had been reading too much Sir Arthur Conan Doyle.

"It's sending a fake signal to the camera so the computer doesn't set off the alarm. This looks like something one of the spy agencies would do."

"I don't think so," said Nikki sniffing around. "There are two sets of footprints, just here. Neither of them is human."

"What are they?"

"Unless I'm wrong, which I'm not, a raccoon and a large monkey."

Jen rolled her eyes, "Oh, brother!"

"What?" Cody asked in confusion.

"Not you, silly... don't you see, it must be Bandit and Chuma," announced Jen.

"Precisely..." started Nikki, but as Jen picked up the radio, it shattered in her hand. Fragments flew into the darkness. There was a terrible yelp. Nikki was down. Cody ran to Nikki and found her bleeding from a hole in her side. She'd been shot and was already going into shock. He placed a hand over the wound to stop the bleeding. "It's all right, old girl," he said. "I'll get you help."

"I don't think so," came a voice. Jen and Cody looked up to see Chuma the Chimpanzee step into their flashlight's beam. She was holding a strange looking weapon, pointed right at them.

"Move away from that dog."

"I will not," said Cody, pulling off his shirt. He tied it around Nikki, using it as a pressure bandage against the bleeding. Nikki groaned.

"Sorry…Co….d..d.d."

"It's all right. Don't move. You'll be fine."

"It will be all right," said Nikki. "I can hear. I can hear them."

"What?"

"I said, move away from the dog," Chuma growled. "I won't say it again," The weapon was now pointing at Jen's head. With a last look at Nikki, Cody stood up and moved back.

"What do you want here?" Cody said, angrily. Chuma laughed.

"We've come to close this prison," she said.

"But we never mistreated you," said Cody.

ZONAUTS

"The Amadorians treat us better," Chuma answered. "After they take over, we'll be in charge."

"You'll be food," Jen groaned. With a snarl, Chuma turned the weapon toward her. A finger tightened on the trigger.

"That's the last you'll ever say, silly girl."

Then a wonderful thing happened. A huge hand came out of the darkness and snatched the weapon away. Chuma was suddenly lifted up. She found herself face to face with Kongo, who was shaking with anger. "Give me one reason why I shouldn't crush you like a melon," he said ferociously.

"Because we don't do that, mate." Coughdrop the Koala stepped out of the darkness and raised his hand. The scene suddenly lit up. There seemed to be a tiny sun hanging overhead. "I found out what I can do," Coughdrop said. "Light and darkness, that's my power."

"Kongo, don't hurt them," said Jen.

"Why not? We found the other one, the raccoon, carrying a bomb. They mean to kill us all."

"Noooo," gasped Chuma. "Not kill. Its a mutagenic bomb. Take away your powers." There came an angry murmur from every animal. Half of Animalville had arrived to help the children,

132

and they weren't in a mood to be nice, but Coughdrop again called for silence.

"Let's think this out, shall we? If we kill these two, don't you think those aliens will just send something worse? Think what we might learn about those space lizards from these henchbeings. But the most important reason is, this isn't who we are. We're the good guys. We gotta fight the way good guys fight: with honor. Now, I never knew your General Mike, but from all I've heard, I don't think he'd approve, do you?" Coughdrop had made his point.

There was a murmur of assent from the animals, and that's when Angie Stroud drove up on the motorized gurney with Mungo, Ham the Chimpanzee and me. Ham and Suzy gently lifted Nikki onto the gurney, Angie checked the bandage Cody had made, and then they sped off to the infirmary. I remained behind. "What'll we do with these two?" Kongo asked.

"Well," said Angie, "They should have some punishment for being out of bed so late."

"No, not Jen and Cody, what about the spies."

"I suppose we should lock them in a storeroom until my husband and Dr. Brooks can question them. We can turn over this gun, and that bomb...say, where is that bomb?"

"I disarmed it," said Miss Baker the Squirrel Monkey, proudly waving her favorite screwdriver.

"You disarmed a mutagenic bomb?" said Cody incredulously.

"We must talk about procedures. That was a very dangerous thing to do," added Angie.

Miss Baker shrugged. "It was a pretty simple bomb, Mrs. Stroud. It looks like they built it from a bunch of old alarm clocks."

Jen looked at Laika, then at me. "Methuselah, what do you think?"

I shrugged. "If they built it the way they build their ships, that would make sense. I just don't understand how any of their junk is able to work. Would it have actually gone off, Miss Baker?"

"I think so," she said. "At about dawn."

"When these two would have been far away," said Cody.

"I think we'd better lock them up now," Kongo concluded.

This turned out to be a tragic mistake, though none of us, not even Chuma the Chimpanzee or Bandit the Raccoon knew it at the time. The two rogue animals were locked in a storeroom and a guard was posted so they couldn't escape. Dr.

Angie removed a crystal pellet from Nikki and announced that the wound was clean and that she would make a full recovery. Some animals went back to bed while others gathered in the saloon to examine the first Amadorian equipment most of us had ever seen.

The gun looked like some cross between a high-tech laser and a medieval blunderbuss with rubber rings and gaskets all over it. We examined each component as Miss Baker pointed out all the reasons it shouldn't work. "It's a mass of solder and screws and things just plugged into other things. There's even a weld, here. These wires look like they wouldn't carry enough electricity to power a toy train, yet they run from the firing mechanism to what must be the battery, this round thing. And this glass tube is not connected to anything but there's a faint purple light glowing in it. Does this thing even work?"

"Ask Nikki," I muttered.

"Oh yeah. Well, I can't tell what it shoots. Light? Heat?"

Cody overturned a small metal tray and a crystal chip rolled out on the table. "Angie took this out of Nikki. The odd thing is that it is twice as big as the hole it made in Nikki."

"Hmmmmm," said Kongo. He picked up a strong magnifying glass and examined the chip closely. "It's a clear symmetrical crystal, faceted like a cut diamond. It seems to be perfect. I...What?"

"What is it Kongo?"

"See for yourself."

"It's grown!" We each took a look through the magnifier. The chip was twice as large. Cody carefully tipped it back into the metal pan.

"If that kept growing inside Nikki, it would have killed her in a matter of hours," Jen realized.

"Well, Dr. Brooks will be here in the morning to collect this, the bomb, and our prisoners. We'll let the government figure out this one," Kongo concluded. We all went to bed, but I don't think anyone slept well that night.

Sixteen: First Contact

In the morning, we got a bad shock. While Nikki was fine, Chuma and Bandit were both dead. There didn't seem to be any cause or reason, they were both just cold. We waited until Dr. Brooks arrived and then he and Dr. Angie performed an autopsy on their bodies. The results were very disturbing.

"We found two little devices, one inside each of them," Dr. Brooks said, "inside both Chuma and Bandit."

"As near as we can tell," said Dr. Brooks, "the Amadorians put them there to control their animal 'friends.' When they hadn't returned by dawn, the devices killed them."

"That's terrible," I said. "But Chuma and Bandit couldn't have known. They never even complained when we locked them up."

"They didn't know," Jen said. "They must have been sacrificed so we couldn't find out anything else."

"See that all the animals know. I want everyone to realize what kind of creatures we're fighting," Kongo announced.

We were talking in the old saloon. Besides Dr. Brooks, Dr. Tom and I, Jen and Cody were

137

there, plus Laika the Dog, Horace the Owl and Suzy the Chimpanzee.

"What do you think the Amadorians will do next?" asked Suzy. "Do you think they'll attack Animalville?"

"They might," said Dr. Brooks. "But remember, there aren't very many of them. They may not want to risk getting killed, or having us get our hands on one of their ships. They might try to capture more animals instead. At any rate, NASA has decided to station an Air Force officer here as head of Security. They'll pick him and he'll arrive in a few weeks.

"And what do we do in the meantime?" I asked. "They can get around our radar. The Air Force can't seem to shoot them down. They could show up here at any moment."

"We may have an answer to that," Hsing-Hsing said, pushing through the door. He was followed by Ling-Ling, who, true to her shy nature, kept behind her mate. "We have discovered what Ling-Ling's power is. But I think we need to go to Kongo's studio to show you."

Kongo was waiting in what he called 'his studio.' It was a large barnlike building that originally housed maintenance equipment for the park, but now was full of blackboards, computers, virtual reality displays and file cabinets. Kongo was waiting for us as we arrived, and greeted each of us solemnly. He took science very seriously, not that he didn't have a sense of humor about other things, but science was his passion.

On the way, Jen grabbed Methuselah by the tail, "just why did you tell Sara so much the other day. I still can't figure that out. The next day after school, she told me a weird dream she had about us..."

"Shhh," Methuselah scolded, "as I told you already Jen, there are things even you don't understand yet. Tell me about the dream later. It could be important, if I'm right about Sara."

When we all were seated, Kongo tapped a few keys on his computer and the center of the room filled with a three-dimensional model of what Kongo referred to as 'near-space.' "Eight light years in every direction," he said. "Our sun is at the center," and as he said this, the star in the center blazed particularly bright. We all oohed and aahed appreciatively.

"I bet even NASA has nothing like this," Cody exclaimed.

"They don't, yet," Kongo said. "I'll be supplying them with the plans, later this month.

ZONAUTS

Hopefully, these will be so cheap to produce that we'll be able to put one in every American school."

"Cool!" Cody replied unconvincingly.

Kongo continued, without acknowledging the interruption, "Now then, here is Amador."

Another light blazed brightly, halfway from our sun to the edge of the display. Then they connected with a flashing green line. "At light speed, 186,000 miles per second—a speed that we cannot even approach, it would take an Amadorian ship about four and a half years to reach Earth. We have reason to believe that they can move far faster than the speed of light."

The room was suddenly a-buzz with talk. Dr. Brooks stood up. "Kongo."

"Yes, Dr. Brooks."

"You said that you have reason to believe that the Amadorians possess a faster-than-light drive. Can you prove this?"

Kongo chuckled, having caught Dr. Brooks in a word trap. "Actually, I said Amadorians can move faster than the speed of light. I never said anything about a drive, or engine."

"Well, if it's not an engine..." began Dr. Brooks, then he suddenly turned and stared at the display. His eyes lit up. "You saw them," he said excitedly. "Engine or not, you saw an Amadorian ship move faster than the speed of light."

"The next best thing," said Kongo. "Ling-Ling?"

Ling-Ling rose and waddled into the center of the room. She is a sweet creature but is as ungainly as a grounded duck. She faced us, and then spoke above her usual shyness. Her English had improved greatly.

"As you know, my mate Hsing-Hsing can read Amadorian minds and memories. When they handled us, he absorbed everything that the two Amadorian pilots—Fishwick and Kornblend—thought, knew or remembered about Amador; experiences, fears, even gossip and legends. We have spent most of our time since we came here recording those memories, so we'll know how to fight them. My power is much simpler. I can detect the mental emanations of Amadorians. I know where they are, and if they are coming toward us or leaving."

"And what is most remarkable," Hsing-Hsing went on, "is that time and space seem to be no barrier to her ability. We used to think that thought traveled at the speed of light, but we had no clear way to measure it. Now we know that, at least in Ling-Ling's case, thought is instantaneous. She can detect Amadorians, on Amador, over four light years away—now."

ZÖNAUTS

There was more buzzing as the animals reacted to that incredible statement. Ignoring them, Kongo handed Ling-Ling a headset. Placing it over her fuzzy white ears, Ling-Ling closed her eyes. Then an amazing thing happened. On the virtual model, there were suddenly lights near the center, near the Earth. Then, after a few seconds, lights blazed up all around Amador. "These lights indicate Amadorians," said Kongo. "Notice a few lights off here and there. We believe that those are scout ships. Watch when I increase the magnification on the Earth and our solar system."

Suddenly the earth was the size of a large marble, with a brilliant basketball-sized sun in the background. "Sorry," muttered Kongo, and turned down the sun's light so that it wasn't so painful. When our eyesight returned, we could see three bright lights around the Earth, one on the Moon, and a cluster of eight or nine some distance away.

"What are those? Amadorians?"

"Yes, mostly in twos. In scout ships we think. We're not exactly sure what this is," Kongo said, indicating the cluster of bright lights.

"Where is that?" asked Cody.

"The asteroid belt, near the asteroid Ceres," said Kongo. "Why? Do you think you know what it is?"

The Secret of Animalville

Cody walked around the model, studying it. "Stop showing off," said his sister, Jen. Cody made a face at her.

"I'm not. That's a forward base, like a death star. That way Amadorian scouts don't have to go all the way back to Amador for hot food and fuel. And baths, if they wash."

"If that's true," I said, "and I think it is, the Amadorians are very serious about wanting the Earth. In World War II, we built forward bases all the way across the Pacific. It's what you do when you want to conquer someone."

"Maybe the Columbia blowing up was an advance attack," suggested Cody.

"It's a little early to say, but the Amadorians could have been involved."

"Then, the only question is, what do we do about it?"

As it turned out, almost the very first thing we did about it was paperwork, which showed that the government was serious. Dr. Brooks handed us each a stack of secrecy agreements, upon which each animal made his or her mark, witnessed by Dr. Brooks and Dr. Tom. The papers said that if we told anyone about anything concerned with Animalville, aliens or the government, we would be placed in prison for the rest of our lives. Some of the animals were offended until I reminded them that we were at war, and had chosen our side. Besides, humans weren't asking anything of us that they weren't asking of each other. Of course, I immediately thought about Sara and all that I told her, so I flew over to Dr. Tom and landed on his shoulder for a private conference.

"Dr. Tom," I whispered, "There is something else that you should know about. A few days ago, Jen told her friend Sara that I could talk. It was sort of an accident, so please don't be angry with her. We met for an emergency Zoonaut council and I was nominated to tell Sara our history."

"But why Methuselah?"

"As we discussed the crisis, Ling-Ling got an image of Sara in her mind. Sara was sleeping on top of a large key. None of us could figure out that vision, but we all decided Sara must be important and should join us. Just before this meeting, Jen told me that Sara had a dream about us, but I don't know yet what it is about."

Dr. Tom turned to his daughter, "Jen, I think we have to talk. Follow me!" As they left the conference room he continued, "It is probably time for you to invite your friend Sara over for a visit." Jen was terrified. Had Methuselah betrayed her?

144

The Secret of Animalville

The alien gun, bomb, and the bodies of Chuma and Bandit were shipped off to some government lab. We never saw them again. In the meantime, we waited for the Amadorians to show up again. Ling-Ling spent much of her time at Kongo's lab, keeping track of the Amadorians. Usually there was one in orbit somewhere above Animalville, probably watching us, though the Air Force could never track it. Whatever the Amadorians used to shield their ships from radar was good.

Then things began to happen that would bring about a face-to-face meeting with the aliens. In March, we decided to send a delegation down to Cape Canaveral in Florida. Jen and Cody would be given a full battery of medical tests and scans to see if growing up with the Animalville gang had changed them. These tests—though they were not to be told this—were also the first tests used to screen potential astronauts.

Kongo's daughter Patty Cake would be going for special tests. Her ability to move herself (psychokinesis) and objects (telekinesis) using only her mental powers was very strong. Dr. Brooks wanted to find out just how powerful she was. She was also going to meet a few NASA officials who needed convincing. Sara had revisited Animalville and repeated her dream to Dr. Tom. Sara had recently had a second unusual dream. She was not sure what it was all about. It

ZoNAUTS

was really a nightmare and in it there was a field of large bulbous pod plants that somewhat resembled Venus Fly Traps. They were planted in a single row straining upward to get a ray of light through a dim unearthly sky. Sara knew instinctively that the plants were dangerous killers although she had no idea where they came from. Their flowers had razor sharp teeth and she awoke in a cold sweat, just as one of them lept at her viciously. Sara even woke up her grandmother Flores with her screams. Was her imagination getting the best of her? Had she watched too many horror movies? She decided to visit Animalville again soon.

Meanwhile, all the exposure bothered Dr. Brooks. As far as he was concerned, too many people knew about Animalville already. As he put it, "Every morning when I open the paper I expect to see them on the front page. If this gets much more out of hand, they'll be hosting the Macy's Christmas Parade."

Finally, the group was to return with the new Chief of Security for Animalville, Major Davis Prescott, US Air Force, who would pilot them back in an Air Force jet. No one had yet briefed Major Prescott about Animalville. We hoped that he would not take the news about us too hard. Meanwhile, the Amadorians had other plans!

Seventeen: Amador

As you may recall from Jen's school report, Fishwick and Kornblend were not happy Amadorians. We left them leaving the Amador Supreme Palace, on the Grand Highway, but perhaps we should fully refresh your memory...

The Grand Highway was a ridiculous name, as the road was merely a thirty-foot wide trench bulldozed out of the dirt so big steam busses could crawl up and down it. The bus that had

recently delivered Fishwick and Kornblend to the Palace had broken down. The Amadorian driver was hitting the boiler with a wrench and calling it names. Fishwick and Kornblend ignored him. They stood under the poisonous yellow sky and stared at the palace.

Calling it a palace was a kindness, though it was certainly large enough. A big ugly rock pile, it reared up against the smoky skies, as if deposited there by a glacier. Amadorian emperors and warlords had been adding to the thing for centuries with no thought to design or architecture. The result was a lumpy

ZONAUTS

building as ugly as any in the galaxy, surrounded by a disreputable city, thick with smoke, machine noises, oil spills and uncollected trash.

Fishwick shook his great scaly head. "I hate this planet!"

Kornblend hooted, blowing the smog out of his snout stops. "But this is our planet."

"I still hate it. In the Amadorian Codex, verse XIII-27, it specifically states that if you lie down with mud weasels, you'll get up smelling like…well, mud weasels, and that's not so good."

"Can we get this over with?" Kornblend whined.

A very old Amadorian Palace Guard leaning on a halberd blaster eyed them suspiciously. His scales were painted in a pattern of bile green and yellow and he looked like he'd been standing there for a hundred years. When he talked, his jaw creaked. "What do you two bozos want?"

"We have an appointment."

"What?"

"We have an appointment."

"What? Speak up. Don't whisper." The old guard was obviously deaf.

"We have an appointment, you old fish-bag!" Kornblend bellowed. "Let us in." Instead, the guard leveled his halberd. Fishwick and

Kornblend looked at each other, then at the guard. The charge light on his blaster was dark and the battery was missing. Fishwick gently pushed the tip aside, then screamed into the oldster's ear.

"Fishwick and Kornblend to see His Awfulness."

"Why didn't you say so?" The guard tossed the useless blaster down and waddled to the intercom. He had to hit it several times before a red light came on. "Fishhead and Kornface are here," he shouted.

With a loud click, the massive doors swung open. Thrusting the guard aside, Kornblend strode through into the palace. With a sigh, Fishwick followed.

The palace interior was no better than outside. Fishwick and Kornblend had been here many times and were used to it.

At the end of the corridor, the two rustic dragons came to a door. In the manner of all soldiers they straightened their uniforms, and in the manner of old partners, they tidied each other up, scowling. "Well, you look like crap."

"Speak for yourself, Kornface"

"Why do you think he wants to see us?"

"Probably to give me a medal," Fishwick growled.

ZONAUTS

"You? What for?"

"For putting up with you, you dumb iguana."

Above, a robot eye swiveled around to look at them. It didn't seem very amused, but then, they never do. Tre-Pok's voice suddenly blasted out from all sides of them. "Fishwick! Kornblend! Get in here!"

Fishwick and Kornblend stumbled into Tre-Pok's Strategy Room, tripping over their tails and going down in a heap. Untangling themselves, they staggered up as Tre-Pok screamed, "Get up!"

The two pilots saluted, Roman-style, thumping their chests. "Yes, Your Awfulness!"

Tre-Pok glared at them. He was decked out in leather, medals and attitude. Some medals were directly attached to his scales. Some scales were covered with shiny metal plates. He examined the two pilots as if he had found them on his boot. "I've got a job for you two mouth-breathers. And I want it done right!"

"Yessir!"

"Silence! You're using up my air." Tre-Pok stalked to his command console, Fishwick and Kornblend trailing behind. He stabbed a button. A huge screen dropped from the ceiling, narrowly missing Fishwick, who gave an involuntary yelp.

The Secret of Animalville

Kornblend clamped his hands around Fishwick's jaws, hoping Tre-Pok hadn't heard, but the High General and Chief Warlord of Amador was busy banging his scaly fist on a projector dome. Suddenly the screen lit up with a picture of Earth. Tre-Pok gave a satisfied grunt. "I want you to go to the Earth..." He rounded on them. "I trust that you remember where it is..."

The two pilots nodded vigorously. Earth faded into Laika the Zoonaut. "And bring back this creature, alive and well."

"Alive and well..." Kornblend repeated. Fishwick elbowed him. "Ow," Kornblend went on. "How do we find her, Your Fearfulness?"

Tre-Pok's angry response frightened them. "Use the genetic sensors we provided you with, bonehead! Do a good job!" He subsided into a large creaking chair and looked at the two quaking pilots. "If you do, there could be medals and another stripe for each of you. If you don't... we might have the same sort of problems here as we did with those blood sucking plants from Veratex."

ZONAUTS

The two turned white, remembering what they had heard about that dreadful blood bath. They saluted so hard they almost broke their breastbones. "Now, get out of here!" Tre-Pok screamed. The two were out the door with a slam before his words finished ringing in the filty air.

Tre-Pok scowled after them, not seeing curtains move behind him as the High Rotocaster slipped in. The Supreme Spiritual Advisor to the Emperor of Amador, the High Rotocaster had been around so long that no one remembered his name, only that he had somehow survived the Veratex disaster. He was now a skeletal, spooky dragon, his scales almost translucent, his eyes red, his voice ethereal—a local equivalent of Hamlet's Ghost. When he cleared his throat, it was like someone eating lightbulbs. Startled, Tre-Pok jumped, then bowed. "Sirrah..."

The High Rotocaster stared distantly in deep thought. He did it all of the time, which drove Tre-Pok crazy. "This had better work..."

Tre-Pok nodded, but Rotocaster's attention is on the picture of Laika. "I must find their weaknesses. We can not afford another mistake."

"I shall not fail the Emperor," Tre-Pok promised, although he secretly had his doubts.

Eighteen: Florida

Major Davis Prescott was not a happy man. He stood at attention before the desk of General Roysmith, the Air Force officer responsible for dealing with NASA. Roysmith was looking through Prescott's file. "You have a first class record, Major."

"Thank you, sir…"

"How long have you been in B-52s?"

Not long enough, thought Prescott, but he answered, "Eighteen months, sir." Then he added. "I was hoping to stay with my current assignment."

"I know you were, Major." Roysmith looked him over. "Relax, Major. At ease."

Prescott slumped slightly. "Why am I being taken out of the Bomb Wing, sir? If there's a problem with my performance—"

"There's no problem, Major Prescott. It's just that we have a new assignment for you. This is a promotion, and make no bones about it, this is a tough job. But do it well and there'll be a gold leaf at the end of it."

A gold leaf. Promotion to Lieutenant Colonel. Prescott groaned. He didn't want a promotion, he wanted to fly.

"Comment, Major?"

"No sir. I mean, yes sir. If it's all the same to the General…"

"No, it isn't," General Roysmith replied, his smile disappearing. "This isn't an offer, it's an order. You will take up the post of Security and Liaison officer at Site Bravo Lucky effective immediately. Do I make myself clear?"

"Yessir."

"Listen, Prescott. This may be the most important security assignment since the Manhattan Project. If this works out, you may have a chance of changing history. Don't take it lightly." He tossed a sealed envelope on the desk. "Your orders."

Prescott picked it up. "Sir."

"Now get out to the flight line."

"The flight line, sir?"

"Yes, you're still a pilot aren't you. Now, scoot. And good luck."

"That was horrible."

"Don't be a baby."

"You're telling me you liked it?"

"No one likes a CAT Scan." Jen and Cody had just finished their NASA physicals. The final event was the 15-minute ride through the noisy vibrating CAT Scan tunnel. Cody was wondering if he might be claustrophobic, but probably not. He just hated having to lie still for fifteen minutes.

"You know what that was for," Jen whispered, as they followed the winding corridors back to the visitor's lounge.

"Yeah. They wanted to see if the animals have changed us. Maybe they thought we were becoming were-monkeys or something," Cody improvised. Jen looked at her brother with tremendous impatience.

"You're such a doofus. What is a 'were-monkey' anyway?

"Some kind of monster, you know, like a werewolf, dah! So really, where and what have you heard?"

Jen had had enough of Cody and was beginning to look for a way to loose him, "No, a nurse told me."

"Told you what?"

"She asked if we'd won some kind of contest. When I told her no, she said, 'You must be important. The full NASA Astronaut physical is very expensive.'"

Cody stopped, dead in his tracks. "Astronaut physical? You're kidding! Right..."

"That's what she said."

"Do you suppose...?

"Why not?"

ZONAUTS

"That's impossible!"

Jen stopped and stared at her brother. "I stopped using the word 'impossible' the first time a talking gorilla helped me with my math and science homework."

Laika and Patty Cake were sitting in a special Security loading area. Patty Cake was eyeing a large metal cage distastefully. "I didn't ride in a cage on the way down."

"No," said Laika, "but Dr. Brooks piloted the plane on the way down. The new Security Officer is flying us back, and he doesn't know about us yet."

"Well, he's certainly going to find out about us when he gets there, isn't he?"

Laika nodded. "Yes, and I expect that it'll be quite a shock to him. He may get nervous, tense, perhaps he may even faint. Now, would you rather have him do that before or after he flies us half way across the United States?"

"After, of course," Patty Cake sulked. "But I still don't like the cage."

"Unfortunately, that's the way things are," Laika reminded her. "Relax. It's only for a few hours, and then we'll be back home."

The Secret of Animalville

A door opened. Jen and Cody walked in. Laika looked up. "Hi, kids. Wanna play frisbee."

"Guess what! They gave us astronaut physicals," said Cody.

"Ah yes, I knew they were going to do that."

"You could have told us."

Laika sat down and scratched thoughtfully. "You weren't supposed to know yet. We may or may not need you to go into space. We don't know how dangerous it will be."

"Cool!"

Jen had a different opinion. "Were they planning to ask us if we wanted to go, or were we going to be drafted?"

"I wanna go!" Cody declared.

"Well, I might want to go to college, or…something else…"

"Or get married?" Jen had been dating a boy from school and Cody loved teasing her about it. "Jen's going to get married to Billy Thurlow and be a housewife," Cody said in a whisper to Laika. "She can't wait."

"I'm sure that if NASA wants any of us to go into space—or go back into space," Laika said with a nod toward Patty Cake—"they will ask us. And if it means saving the planet, I for one, will go."

"Me too," said Cody.

"And me," declared Patty Cake.

"Well, I shall think it over," Jen declared. "If they ask me."

With a whir of motors, the great hangar doors began to roll back. Laika shooed Patty Cake back into her cage and latched it, as bright lights flooded the loading area. Outside stood a sleek executive jet. Men came in to push Patty Cake's cage toward the plane, as Jen, Cody and Laika walked alongside.

There was a man standing by the doorway to the plane in the uniform of an Air Force major. He must be the new Security Officer, Jen and Cody decided. He was holding a clipboard.

"Jennifer and Cody Stroud?" he asked.

"That's Jen and Cody. And this is Laika." Laika sat at Jen's heel, looking like a normal dog. "And that is Patty Cake."

Major Prescott turned to see the men pushing a cage from the lift into the cargo door of the plane. Inside, a disgruntled-looking Patty Cake looked back at him.

"I'm going to have a huge monkey on my plane?" the Major said in angry disbelief.

"Not a monkey," said Jen, "a gorilla, and she's very…ummm, calm."

"She doesn't look calm," said Prescott, grinding his teeth.

"Neither do you, and you're flying the plane," Cody said under his breath. Prescott looked at him with disdain.

"What?"

"Nothing. Can we go aboard?" Prescott nodded, then watched as the kids and Laika boarded the plane. He shook his head. What crazy deal had he gotten himself into this time?

Major Prescott flew them west across the Florida panhandle, toward Houston. Between them and Animalville, a large storm was gathering itself above the Mississippi River delta. Huge thunderheads and storm clouds were rearing up above the land and moving south, out into the Gulf of Mexico. The little executive jet was heading straight into it.

Major Prescott was at the controls, letting the plane fly itself, listening to the weather report with half an ear. Sitting next to him in the co-pilot seat was Cody, who was far too young to be a pilot, but he had talked the Major into giving him a flight lesson. Major Prescott watched the developing storm. He was bored, and even a little resentful. He glanced at Cody at the controls next to him.

"Easy on the stick, son. She'll fly herself if you let her. That's the way she's built." He glanced out the window. Biloxi, Mississippi was far below them. Clouds covered much of the Gulf. "Some job for a decorated combat pilot."

"You don't like working for N.A.S.A?"

Prescott glanced at Cody. "As what? An air taxi driver for a bunch of zoo animals? Fooey!"

"They're not zoo animals," Cody said stubbornly. "They're all NASA spaceflight veterans!" Prescott scowled, unconvinced of his good fortune. "Hey, Major, cheer up. Maybe they'll let you fight a war somewhere."

"That's not funny," the Major said. "You shouldn't joke about things like that."

"Duh! Lighten up…sir."

Kids! Major Prescott thought. Kids and animals. I wonder if I can transfer to the Navy.

Back in the passenger and cargo compartment, Jen Stroud and Laika were sitting on opposite facing seats, looking out of the window, when the FASTEN SEATBELTS sign came on. Lightning flashed outside and Jen cringed. "I hate flying through storms."

"Modern air travel is relatively safe in any weather," Laika said thoughtfully. "Now, if you

The Secret of Animalville

want a frightening flight, I recommend high angle orbital re-entry. Very nasty."

Jen shuddered at the thought. "I'll pass for now." She look at Patty Cake, who was curled up morosely in her large cage. "Are you okay?"

"I hate this cage," she whined. "Why can't I sit on the seat? Laika's on the seat."

"Because I'm a dog. Dogs sit on seats. Major Prescott doesn't know about us. Humans are afraid of gorillas. You saw King Kong."

"King Kong was framed!"

A bolt of lightning rocked the plane, causing all three of them to cry out in surprise. Then the intercom buzzed, startling Jen a second time. It was Cody's voice.

"Cool storm, huh? You okay back there?"

"No," Jen cried. "I'm not. I hate storms. Can't we go around it?"

"No way, Sis, but we can go over it. Hang on." The intercom went dead.

"Hang on?" Patty Cake exclaimed. "What does he mean, hang on?" At that moment, they felt the plane begin to climb. Patty Cake gripped the bars of her cage and gritted her teeth.

"I still hate storms!" Jen shouted.

But as the jet swiftly rose above the clouds, something larger, rounder and more menacing

161

was flying above it -- something invisible to their radar—an Amadorian spacecraft.

"It's them!   It's them!" Kornblend yelped. Crammed in the little cockpit, amid gauges, lights, dial, levers, wheels, food wrappers and Earth magazines, the two Amadorians were trying to line up their range finders on the jet. Fishwick fought the controls.   The storm was bouncing the ungainly scout ship around.

"Are you sure?' Fishwick asked. Kornblend thumped a piece of equipment with a lighted screen in the side. The screen flickered, then the picture came back.

"Be careful," Fishwick ordered.   "That equipment is delicate."

"Right. Well, it says that the dog creature Laika is in that plane. Get in closer! I'll blast them."

"You idiot! We're supposed to bring the dog back alive and well. The Big Lizard wants to study it."

Kornblend looked at his partner, his mind turning over this incomprehensible idea. "Why?"

"So they can learn how to take over the Earth..."

"Oh...Why not just blast the Earth?"

"Because," Fishwick said patiently, "if we do, the Earth will wind up looking like our planet, you bonehead."

A light seemed to go on behind Kornblend's dense forehead. "Oh... good reason. I'll just target their engines."

"You do that."

As the little jet pulled out above the clouds, they hit calmer air and the plane leveled off. Major Prescott decided to call in. "Houston, this is NASA One-Niner. We are one hour out. Request landing clearance, over."

Just at that moment, about a half-mile above them, Kornblend was peering into his targeting scope. As he pressed the trigger, he spoke in heavily-accented English words that had become his own battle cry. "*Hasta la vista*, baby!"

A beam of electrical energy lanced down, hitting the jet engines. Inside the cockpit of NASA One-Niner, Prescott and Cody ducked away as the plane was suddenly bathed in brilliant light.

"What was that? Lightning?"

But Prescott had heard the bang as the engines blew out. "I don't think so." All of the dials dropped to zero and alarms began going off. He grabbed for the controls. "Something hit us! We've got no engines! Buckle up and hang on!"

ZONAUTS

Major Prescott wrestled the controls as the plane nosed over and started dropping fast. Cody grabbed for the radio microphone. "Houston, this is NASA One-Niner. We're going down!" He looked at the Major. "Where are we going down?"

"The Atchafalaya Swamp, somewhere east of New Iberia." As Cody repeated that into the radio, they hurtled down through the thundering clouds, toward the bayous below.

In the rear compartment, Patty Cake was hanging on to the bars of her cage, as Jen clutched her seat belt and Laika slid up against the forward bulkhead. "I thought you said this was safe!" cried Jen.

"I said 'relatively' safe!" Laika replied. He was upside down against the cabin wall.

Cody and Major Prescott were watching as the plane suddenly dropped below the clouds, screaming low over the Louisiana Bayou. They were passing trees that were higher than they were. "It's gonna be a water landing," said the Major through clenched teeth. And, just missing a huge tree, NASA One-Niner belly-landed on the water, throwing roostertails of spray as it skipped like a stone toward the forest.

"Yaaaaaaaaahhhh!" The plane shot between two trees, clipping off the wings, and came to rest in a tree-shaded pool, where it started to sink... A few seconds later, the Amadorian spacecraft cruised by overhead, searching for the plane. "I don't see it."

"Keep looking. It's got to be here somewhere."

The Amadorian spacecraft disappeared over the trees. The plane, its cargo door open, was slowly filling with water. Nearby, Major Prescott, Jen, Cody, Laika and Patty Cake, were huddling out of the rain on a tiny one-tree island. Prescott looked around. "We'll be all right now. The plane has a radio transponder. It should lead them right to us."

"If that freak bolt of lightning didn't knock it out," said Cody. "If it was lightning." Prescott looked at Cody.

"Yeah. Well, kid, if it knocked out the transponder it probably knocked out the cockpit radio too, which means that no one heard our distress call."

"Rats."

Patty Cake saw something. Tapping Jen on the shoulder, they turned in time to see an Amadorian ship cruise by a hundred yards away. Jen looked at Patty Cake. "Is that what I think it is?" Patty Cake nodded. They were lost in a swamp, in the rain, with space monsters after them. She only wished to be back in her clean dry cage.

ZONAUTS

Nineteen: In Animalville

The same storm that was drenching the Louisiana swamp was just starting to move through Texas. The sky was almost black and the first few raindrops were beginning to fall on the streets of Animalville. Most of the animals headed inside to get out of the rain, but a few, like the frogs and toads, came out to enjoy the shower. Inside the lighted windows of the Stroud Veterinary Clinic, there were happy puppy noises.

Tom was examining a small husky/shepherd puppy named Laika Junior. Junior was reacting with enthusiastic affection to Tom's attention, wiggling and woofling. His mother, Heisler, watched proudly from the couch.

"Good boy. Good Junior. Too bad Jen and Cody aren't here to see you." Tom turned to Heisler. "He's just fine."

Heisler wagged her tail. "That's good. His daddy will be so pleased." She wrinkled her brow in concern. "I wish he was here too."

"They all will be back in a few hours and should even arrive before suppertime. The new security officer is flying them in from Florida."

Heisler laughed. "Is he going to be in for a shock!"

Dr. Tom set Junior back on the floor. He bustled back to his mom and hopped up on the couch. "Perhaps Dr. Brooks briefed him before he left."

"Even if he did," Heisler said, "it'll still be a shock." Junior yipped and wiggled as Heisler played with him. "Where's Dr. Angie tonight?"

"She's in Washington, attending a conference on endangered animal species."

Heisler laughed, and Junior yipped and butted her with his head. "If the aliens have their way, we'll all be endangered," she said.

Across the room, Mungo the Parrot sat before a computer console, playing a lightning fast game of 'Tetris,' pecking like a machine, and not missing a block. Luna the Cat paused in grooming herself to give him a disapproving look.

"You spend far too much time in front of that thing. You're going to ruin your eyes," she said.

"Ha!" squawked Mungo. "The future is electronic. This is the e-tech age."

"Perhaps, but you're going to look funny wearing glasses."

The phone rang and Tom picked it up. "Clinic, Tom Stroud. Yes? Where?"

Everything in the clinic stopped as the animals caught the worried tone in Dr. Tom's voice and turned to listen . "Can you tell me anything else? Okay, thank you..."

Hanging up, Dr. Tom turned to Mungo. "Mungo. Get Kongo, now!"

"Trouble, chief?"

"The kids' plane went down. Hurry!"

A hundred feet below, in the parking garage, Sarafina Flores-Abaroa was parking her bike. She had to tell someone about her most recent dream. Sara was still shaken by the image of a plant leaping at her. Then, holding her precious Security Pass, which she'd just gotten only ten days earlier, she walked toward the elevator thinking about how much her life had changed, forever. After another guard examined the pass, she got into the elevator.

Mungo was out the door like a shot. He flew between raindrops as he streaked across the main street of Animalville, passing two curious Chimps in raincoats, riding their bicycles.

He entered the Arcade, zooming past Horace the Owl, making him drop his newspaper, and causing him to squawk in irritation.

Flying on he entered the old Funhouse ride, where the primates now made their homes, looking around frantically. "The plane's gone down... The plane!" he yelped, then realized that he was talking to himself. He looked around. Gina the Orangutan was welding a freestanding metal sculpture. She pushed back her welder's helmet and turned off the torch, as Mungo zoomed up and hovered in front of her face. "Where's Kongo?"

"Where he always is. In his lab."

"Thankya, Thankya very much!" Mungo drawled in his best Elvis imitation, and flew off.

"Silly bird," mumbled Gina, as Ham the Chimpanzee stuck his head out of a bathroom, his mouth full of toothpaste, a toothbrush stuck in his face.

"What was that all about?" he said trying not to drool toothpaste.

"I dunno. Something about a plane crash."

"WHAT!?" Ham exploded, spraying water and toothpaste over everything. Before Gina could say anything, he too was gone.

In the center of the Kongo's lab, dozens of lighted particles circled through the air, forming a complex theoretical matrix. It was a holographic representation of Kongo's latest theory. It was also quite pretty.

ZONAUTS

Kongo, the huge silverback gorilla, who with Laika, led Animalville, stood watching the matrix, while adjusting it on a small hand-held keyboard. Occasionally, he paused to poke his glasses back onto his flat nose. "Ummmmmm," he said. Then, "hmmmm uh huh." He turned to chalk down some numbers and symbols on a blackboard.

At that moment, Mungo flew in and perched on the end of a telescope, which dropped under his weight, nearly hitting the table it stood on.

"Be careful of that," Kongo growled. "It's delicate."

"*De Plane, Boss...De Plane!*" Mungo shrieked.

Kongo's attention was still on the lighted matrix. "What are you babbling about?"

Catching his breath, Mungo dropped back into his normal voice. "The plane, the one coming back from Florida... with the kids! It's...gone down in a swamp."

"WHAT!" Kongo bellowed, involuntarily crushing the keyboard. As he did, all of the moving specks of light stopped, fell, and went out as they hit the floor.

A moment later the outer wall of the old Maintenance Building which housed Kongo's lab bulged, then exploded outward, as Kongo ran through it, heading for the airstrip, followed by

Mungo flying behind him. A few seconds after that, Ham the Chimpanzee, still streaked with toothpaste, appeared in the opening where the wall used to be.

"Hey, wait for me!"

On the airstrip, a big heavy-lift copter was warming up. Its door opened. The pilot was an Orangutan named Percy, but since he'd learned to fly, he insisted that everyone call him Race, after a cartoon character. Tom didn't mind, Race was a terrific pilot. Coughdrop, a radio headset squashed down over his bush hat, sat in the co-pilot's chair. He was learning to fly from Race, though his small koala arms and legs needed mechanical extenders to reach the controls.

Tom was waiting by the door. Mungo flew past him, squawking, "Here he comes!", into the copter, as Kongo ran up. Tom joined his friend.

"Now don't panic. Spysat One has their plane pinpointed. We'll get them out." Kongo was close to having a full gorilla meltdown, but he controlled his voice well, considering...

"Considering that my only daughter is lost in a swamp, I think I'm being remarkably calm."

"Hey, wait for me." Tom and Kongo turned as Ham ran up to them.

"Just what we need," Kongo groaned, not at all happy to see the gangly teenaged Chimp. "What are you doing here?"

"If Patty Cake's in trouble, I'm going."

"No, you're not!" Kongo bellowed, but Tom got the last word.

"Kongo, we need Ham. His abilities may come in handy."

Kongo looked angrily at Ham, who stood his ground and stuck out his jaw. Kids! He thought. How do we survive them? "Very well. But if he does anything—"

"I won't!" cried Ham, as he hurried into the copter, followed by Tom and Kongo.

"Wait!" Tom turned to see Sara riding up on one of the base bicycles, followed by Gina the Orangoutan, two chimps and Horace the Owl.

"I want to help," cried Sara, "and there is something I have to tell you. I had another dream and it really scared me!"

"We have no time to talk now," said Tom. "This mission is off-limits to civilians." Tom looked at Sara, who seemed so desperate to be doing something important. "Go back to the clinic and take care of Heisler. She just had pups. You're in charge until we get back," he said, with a wink at

Gina. Then he hopped aboard the copter, which rocketed straight up into the dark sky.

Sara stood watching them go, bitterly disappointed, until Gina put her long arm around her shoulder.

"Oh Gina, won't anyone listen to me?"

"Yes honey, I'm here. Now what is this dream all about? Did you eat something weird before bedtime? That always gives me bad dreams."

"No, I think it is something that is going to happen, or maybe it already happened, or... I don't know!" said Sara in a jumbled confusion.

"Well, come on," said Gina the Orangoutan. "Tell me all about it and maybe we can figure something out. Meanwhile, let's see what we can do to help with this new Heisler puppy, Junior."

ZöNAUㅌ

Twenty: Down Boondocks

With a Blurping noise, the tail of NASA One-Niner disappeared under the surface of the dirty swamp water. The little plane was gone. "Hope they don't take that out of your pay," Cody muttered to Major Prescott.

"I didn't blow the engines out of that plane," the Major replied gloomily. "Something hit us."

"Not lightning?"

"No way."

As the rain pelted down, the five survivors huddled under their single tree, trying to stay dry, Major Prescott staying as far away from Patty Cake as he could. Jen turned to Cody and whispered, "We've got to do something. There are Amadorians out there looking for us."

"What?"

"Patty Cake and I saw one of their scout ships a few minutes ago."

"Oh, no..." Cody slumped down against the tree trunk. "Now what?" He felt Laika's paw on his arm, and looked into the dog's questioning eyes. Putting his lips near Laika's ear, Cody passed on the bad news.

The Secret of Animalville

"Why are you whispering to a dog?" asked Major Prescott.

"Because it's a secret," Cody said flippantly, hoping the Major would take him for being a wise guy and not push it.

"A secret?"

"Yeah."

"To a dog?"

"That's right."

"Dogs can't talk."

"Then he probably won't tell anyone," said Cody. Prescott scowled and bit back a reply. Then he shook his head.

"Well, someone has to do something." The Major began to get to his feet, pulling out his service pistol.

"Whoa, Major, what are you going to do with that?" asked Jen.

"I'm going to fire a few shots. Maybe someone will hear it and come get us."

Jen jumped to her feet. "I have a better idea. Patty Cake, can you climb this tree and see if you can tell where we are?"

Patty Cake looked at her, nodded, and climbed up and out of sight. The Major was watching this dubiously. "What can she tell us if she does? She's a monkey!"

ZONAUTS

Laika rolled his eyes. Offended, Jen snapped, "She's a gorilla! And a very smart one." Major Prescott threw up his hands.

"My mistake. That makes all the difference."

Patty Cake climbed to the top of the tree, but instead of looking around, she closed her eyes and touched a finger to her temple. Instantly, one of her powers became active, for, unlike the other animals, Patty Cake had more than one ability. There was no telling how many—the Strouds and Kongo were still trying to determine just how gifted she was—but one of them was an ability to Far-See, to see a person or an object that was too far away or out of sight by knowing what to look for. And Patty Cake had seen the Amadorian ship cruise by. She knew what to look for.

As she focused in, each vision narrowing the distance by half, the scene wavered and the colors washed out to gray. Then, with a blur of speed, there suddenly appeared a dot of brilliant color. With a blink she halved the distance again and the object focused in her mind to reveal the Amadorian spacecraft, sitting on a small island. Patty Cake, her eyes still closed, frowned.

"From bad to worse," she murmured. "What next?"

The Secret of Animalville

On that island in Patty Cake's vision, the Spacecraft was sitting inexpertly camoflaged with moss and branches. The door opened, and out stepped Fishwick and Kornblend, now decked out as foot soldiers; carrying battle lasers, and wearing body armor that made them look like rejects from a Road Warrior movie. Fishwick was furious and turned a withering glance at his partner.

"I can't believe you shot it down."

"I just targeted the engines like you said,' said Kornblend, sulking.

"Then how come it didn't hover?"

"Maybe Earth ships don't hover."

"Don't be ridiculous," replied Fishwick. "They must hover. We've seen Earth ships hover. If they don't hover, how can they loiter? Or lurk?" Fishwick kicked at a hummock of earth, but merely scattered mud on his leg.

Kornblend powered up his laser and tried to look fierce. "Their ship crashed over there. Let's just go get the dog."

"What if the dog isn't alone?" considered Fishwick. "What if there are others?"

"We got no orders about others."

Fishwick's mood brighten considerably. "In that case, we can eat them. Remember what the Amadorian Codex says, VII-39. 'The friend of

177

your enemy is your enemy as well, and if he is your enemy you may eat him as well, preferably in a nice light wine sauce.' I wonder how they taste. I'm getting awfully tired of dried frinkfruit and iguana jerky."

"We can eat them then?"

"Yes."

"Good." Kornblend brandished his laser threateningly, and said in his best Clint Eastwood imitation (which wasn't very good), "Do you feel lucky...punk?" His long-suffering partner shook his head.

"You have got to stop watching Earth movies. Come on."

And, loaded for trouble, they waded off the island, heading for the downed plane.

Major Prescott leaned against the tree, getting wetter and more impatient. Looking at the pool where the plane had gone down, he didn't see Patty Cake lower herself out of the tree and drop to the ground behind him.

"This is getting us nowhere," he grumped. Patty Cake chose that moment to tap him on the shoulder, causing him to almost jump out of his clothes. "Don't do that!" he said, backing away, but Jen, Cody and Laika crowded around.

"What did you see?" Jen asked.

Patty Cake glanced uncomfortably at Prescott, shrugged, and then began an elaborate attempt at Sign Language. Prescott, his eyes still on Patty Cake, bent down to Cody. "What's she saying?"

"I have no idea," Cody said. "Jen, this isn't working."

Jen looked helplessly at Laika, who shrugged and gave up the deception. "Patty, perhaps you had better deliver your report verbally."

Major Prescott's eyes grew as large as quarters, not believing what he had just witnessed. "A talking dog? What is this, a trick?" He turned on Cody angrily. "This is no time for games. How did you do that?"

Patty Cake sighed. "He didn't. I'm a ventriloquist."

"The monkey too?" Prescott cried.

"Gorilla!" came the chorus. Jen smothered a laugh as she remembered Sara's first reaction to Methuselah. Laika and Cody confronted Prescott.

"These animals are special: Top Secret. That's why they chose you to guard them."

"We wanted the best," Laika said. "They were going to tell you in Houston. I'm sorry to have startled you..."

ZONAUTS

Prescott waved his hand absently, still not believing a word of it. "Nah, that's okay..." He backed away until his shoes were under water, but he didn't seem to notice. Laika stepped up to Patty Cake.

"Patty Cake, what did you see?"

"There's an Amadorian spacecraft down on an island near here, and there are two of their soldiers headed this way."

"They must be the ones who shot us down."

Cody grinned. "See Major, they won't take it out of your pay."

Jen suddenly had an inspiration, "This is all just like Sara's dream!"

"What dream?" asked Laika and Patty Cake in unison.

"You know, my best friend Sara. Well she had a dream the night after Methuselah told her about us. We were all lost in a swamp being chased by smelly monsters. The only way we survived was by Patty Cake using her mind control somehow."

"Could it work?" Laika asked Patty Cake.

"Maybe, but I'd need to have some powerful object to focus on and it has to be something I know how to use. Swamp trees won't do. Maybe we can capture something the aliens have."

Prescott suddenly noticed that he was standing in water and stepped back on the island. He shook off his foot. "Hey, talking animals is one thing, but you're not going to get me to believe that there are aliens out there."

And, as if right on cue, a laser blast hit the tree above them, bringing down leaves and branches on their heads. Cody grabbed Prescott by the arm. "Argue later, run now."

Patty Cake, Laika and the kids floundered into the water, heading for the next island. Prescott, still not buying it, ducked as another blast sliced through the trees. "There's got to be an explanation for all this," he said to himself.

A large branch crashed to the ground at his feet. "This is nuts!" he decided, but he was running as fast as the rest.

ZONAUTS

Twenty-one: Sky Above and Mud Below

The big heavy lift helicopter was roaring low over the swamp. Lightning forked down in the distance. Tom watched it as it struck around New Iberia, to the north. Race was flying the copter with a practiced touch. Coughdrop sat beside him with a clipboard, taking notes.

"Race, when we get down, I want you to stay with the copter."

"Roger, skipper," the Orangutan said easily. He was holding the control yoke with his feet. Tom decided that he'd never get used to that. He tapped Coughdrop on the shoulder.

"You too. Stay with the ship."

"Too right," Coughdrop replied. "Koalas aren't built for mucking about in the swamp."

Tom reached for the intercom. "Kongo, would you come up here please?"

Kongo squeezed through the doorway into the cockpit. "Yes, doctor?"

Tom indicated a screen in the cabin console. It was a shot of the bayou, with lighted silhouettes indicating the plane and something else. "Spysat

ZONAUTS

One is over the bayou now. It's pinpointed the plane, but what is that thing?"

Kongo groaned, then snorted angrily. "That, I fear, is an Amadorian scout ship."

"So, I'm finally going to get to see an Amadorian."

"Well, according to Hsing-Hsing and Coughdrop, I'm afraid they're not much to look at."

"How is the team holding up?" Tom asked. Kongo rolled his eyes.

"I'll be amazed if they don't all get lost within the first five minutes."

In back of the copter, the rest of the team—Ham, Mungo and Luna were bouncing along as the copter passed through the trailing edge of the storm. Mungo was trying out his best John Wayne accent.

"All right, listen up people. When we hit the L.Z., I want you to keep your eyes open, stay alert, and watch out for Charlie..."

Ham looked at Luna. "Charlie?"

Luna was licking her paws. She looked up, then glanced at Mungo. "He lives in a world of his own."

184

Mungo had switched and was now imitating Bill Paxton in 'Aliens.' "Is this a stand-up fight or just another bug-hunt?"

Luna looked at Ham. "If he keeps this up, can I eat him?"

"No." Ham looked miserable.

"Worried about Patty Cake?"

"Yes. If anything happened to her, I'd..." Ham paused, seething with anger. "I don't know what I'd do. When I get my hands on whoever did this, I'll..."

Ham hadn't seen Kongo return. The huge Silverback leaned down toward him. "You'll do what you're told. That's my daughter out there, and the doctor's children, with Laika. If you do anything to endanger them..."

"I wouldn't do that," Ham declared. "I love Patty Cake!"

Kongo grabbed Ham and pulled him up very close. "Love? You're just a child. You should be home. You—" Kongo broke off, frustrated and angry, trying to control the rage he felt. "My daughter is too young to be dating... a teenaged flying monkey."

Ham stared right back into Kongo's angry eyes. "You watch. I'll save her."

Disgusted, Kongo turned away and stared at the wall. Ham looked at Luna. "Cheer up, kid,"

Luna said. "Romeo and Juliet had it rough at first too."

Ham didn't seem comforted by this. "Romeo and Juliet died."

Luna shrugged. "Oh. Yeah. Forget I mentioned it."

It was early spring, dusk and overcast heavily with clouds, and all of those things combined to make the Louisiana bayou a dark and scary place. Jen and Cody were very happy to slog out of the wet onto a patch of grass at the edge of a road. They were soaked to the skin and getting cold.

Across the road was what appeared to be a rockin' Roadhouse. There was no name on the building, but neon signs advertised ROADHOUSE and EATS and DRINKS, and strings of lights on poles edged the parking lot, which was filled mostly with pickup trucks and motorcycles. Zydeco music was blaring out into the dark, and the smells of shrimp and catfish had been drawing them in this direction for the last half hour.

"Civilization!" Cody cried. He scrambled up and started toward the Roadhouse, but Laika and Jen tackled him, bringing him down. A truck screamed past, roaring down the road at eighty miles an hour, missing him by inches.

"Wow. Thanks."

Laika looked at him severely. "How many times have I told you to look both ways before crossing?"

"Got it," Cody said, backing away from the road. As he did, Major Prescott waded out of the muck. He stopped, seeing the kids and Laika, then looked around.

"Where's the monkey?"

"Gorilla!" Jen snapped. "I thought she was with you.

"And I thought she was with you. Rats!"

"This is weird... it's just like Sara's dream! We'll have to go back," said Jen.

"No way."

"But if Sara's dream is true, we need Patty Cake to get us out of this alive! We—" Just then, a way off in the swamp behind the closest trees, came the zap and sizzle of laser fire.

"Bad idea," Prescott said. "We need to get you kids to safety, then I'll come back for the m...gorilla."

"But..."

"No buts, kid. My job is to take care of the animals. I can't do that if I have to watch you. Forget the dreams, we use our wits instead. Come on, I have an idea."

Looking both ways, they scrambled across the road into the parking lot. There, among the parked trucks, cars and motorcycles, the smell of food was much stronger, almost irresistable. Prescott started trying the doors of the nearest trucks. The third one he tried was unlocked. He opened the door.

"Get in." Laika and the kids piled into the cab of the large red pickup truck, as Prescott popped the hood and began looking for the right wires. Cody leaned out of the cab.

"Isn't this stealing?"

"That's what I was gonna ask." Prescott turned to see a huge bearded man in greasy dungarees and a leather jacket looking at him. The man was holding a pool cue like a club. Prescott swallowed hard.

"US Government," he said. "We need this truck."

"You a cop?"

"Air Force."

"What's the Air Force need with a truck?" the man said. Laika stuck his head out of the cab.

"Actually, we're borrowing it. As a military officer, the Major has the right to commandeer civilian transport in times of war."

The man looked at Laika, his eyes widening. "A talking dog. Cool." He scratched his wooly head. "You mean those Iraqis are right here in Louisiana!"

At that moment a laser blast shot out of the swamp and hit the Roadhouse's highway sign, bringing it down with a crash and sparks.

"Sorry I asked," the man said, and ran for it, adding, "It ain't my truck anyhow." Just then the engine roared to life. Major Prescott slammed the hood, jumped into into the cab, and peeled out of the gravel lot onto the road.

Moments later Fishwick and Kornblend came up out of the swamp. Fishwick was consulting the life detector, while Kornblend looked around for something else to shoot with his laser. Suddenly he saw the Roadhouse.

"Outstanding!."

"Leave it alone," said Fishwick. "I'm getting confusing readings. There's a lot of Earth things in there, and some more that way," he said, gesturing after the lights of the pickup truck, disappearing down the highway.

"Where are the most things?"

"In the building."

"All right then," Kornblend growled, shifting into his Bruce Willis mode. He held the laser high across his chest, and marched toward the Roadhouse, intoning solemnly, "Yippee Ki-Yay!"

Fishwick shrugged, and followed his fellow Amadorian straight into trouble.

As Fishwick and Kornblend stepped into the Roadhouse, everything stopped. Fifty or sixty bikers, oil riggers, fishermen and their girlfriends stared at the two dragons. The dragons stared back. Then Kornblend, seized by the odors of cooking fish, stalked to the fryer and emptied the contents, grease and all, into his mouth. "Mmmmmmmmmmm."

The cook stepped up to Kornblend, his fists clenched. "Who gone pay for dat fish, you big ugly lizard, you?"

Kornblend looked at him and let out a huge burp, smelling of fish, grease and the horrible smells that normally lived in the Amadorian stomach. The cook staggered back, then leaned into a roundhouse right, hitting Kornblend as hard as he could in the schnoz. Kornblend just looked at him, his eyes narrowing angrily.

"No good can come of this," Fishwick said, shaking his head. Then Kornblend raised his laser and blew the roof off the building, and all of the humans ran for it.

Prescott, the kids and Laika—all stuffed into the front seat of the pickup—were tearing down the road at high speed, thinking they would at least make a temporary getaway. It was disturbing how easily the Amadorians were able to follow them. It was almost as if they could read their minds.

"How do we get back to Patty Cake?" Jen asked.

Major Prescott had worked that out. "First, I leave you kids with the cops in the nearest town, or whatever, and then that dog here and I—"

"My name is Laika."

"Sorry. Then Laika and I retrace our steps. Simple, right? Let's go!"

But Cody was looking in the rearview mirror. "Sounds like a plan, but there may be a problem."

Prescott looked in the mirror. There was a big tricycle motorcycle, coming on fast. Fishwick was piloting, with Kornblend and his laser sitting up behind. Both were now wearing biker vests over their armor. Prescott slammed his fist angrily on the dashboard.

"They're faster than we are, and they've got that blasted laser gun."

"Well, floor it!" Jen shouted.

Major Prescott pushed the gas pedal to the floor. The pickup shot down the darkened highway well over the speed limit. Fortunately, they were on official government business.

ZONAUTS

On the tricycle, Fishwick sat, hunched over the handlebars, trying to ignore the wind screaming past him. He blew a bug out of one of his nasal flaps and yelled, "This Earth machine isn't safe."

But Kornblend was having entirely too much fun. "Faster! Faster! This is exciting. We're going to be heroes. I'm your worst nightmare!"

"Any faster and we'll be dead heroes!" groaned Fishwick. Just then Kornblend fired his laser weapon. The shot went off so close to his head, that Fishwick thought he'd been hit.

"Yaaaaaaaaah!"

"What?"

"You hit me!"

"Did not! Don't be such an egg. Arnold would never say that."

Fishwick was furious. "I am not Arnold Whatshisnegger. You are not Arnold Whatshisnegger. Now just shoot that vehicle!"

The first laser shot had gone into the forest. The next slagged a hole in the highway alongside the speeding pickup truck.

"That was too close," Major Prescott said.

"Perhaps there's something I can do," said Laika. He wriggled through the cab window and into the bed of the pickup. He looked over the tailgate. The motor-trike was getting closer.

Kornblend fired again. This time the shot was right on target...but a glistening force bubble appeared, deflecting and scattering the laser light.

Kornblend's eyes narrowed. "I hit it. How'd they do that? Do Earth speeders have force fields?"

"It's the dog ... the one we want," cried Fishwick. "He's doing it. Shoot again."

Kornblend fired again.

In the bed of the pickup, Laika saw the laser glow again and concentrated. A silver force bubble formed around the rear of the pickup, just as the laser light hit it, scattering again.

Jen and Cody were looking through the rear window of the cab. "That was cool! Yea, Laika!"

Jen punched her brother's arm. "Yeah, cool, but how long can he keep it up?"

In the back, Laika realized that Jen was right. There were only so many times he could cast that force bubble before his energy was gone.

In the cab, Major Prescott concentrated on the road ahead. Suddenly brilliant searchlights stabbed down out of the darkness, bathing the road in light. "Now what?"

More searchlights struck the vehicle, and the air suddenly filled with flying debris and a huge woooosh of air. "We're trapped!" the Major yelled, as he jammed on the brakes.

The pickup went skidding to a stop as a lighted, glowing craft dropped the road in front of them. Prescott, Jen and Cody were frozen in their seats, trying to see against the glaring light when the Cody recognized the craft in front of them. "Well, I'll be—"

"We're saved!" cried Jen.

"Saved?" Prescott asked.

The lights shifted so that they could see a big heavy lift helicopter on the road in front of them, with Kongo standing in the open doorway.

On the moto-trike, the Amadorian had also seen the helicopter. "It's an Earth ship!" Kornblend screamed. "Stop this thing!"

But Fishwick was banging on the handlebars. He had no idea where the brakes were. "Sure! How?"

"Turn it."

Fishwick turned the handlebars...

Now, every Earth child knows that if you're riding a tricycle fast and you turn the handlebars, you're going to have an accident, but apparently they didn't have tricycles on Amador. The front wheel suddenly locked, and the moto-trike and its riders went cartwheeling end over end into the darkness of the swamp. "Yaaaaaaaaahhh!"

ZONAUTS

For a moment there was no sound, and then a huge splash in the swamp. After a second, Fishwick screamed, "This is all your fault."

Back on the road, Tom jumped out of the copter and ran to embrace his kids. "Wow, am I glad to see you. Are you all right?"

"We're okay, Dad. Chill out. Uh oh..."

Major Prescott was staring in shocked surprise at Kongo, who was looking around for Patty Cake. Laika stepped up to Kongo.

"Where's my daughter?"

"Now, don't get upset, old friend..."

But Kongo was a gorilla, and gorillas have a temper. "Patty Cake!" he screamed. "Where is she?" He began to pound the road, putting holes in the asphalt. The others watched nervously.

Ham stepped out of the copter. "I'll bring her back," he said.

"Not a word from you," Kongo warned. Then he turned to Prescott. "And who are you?"

"I'm Major Davis Prescott. I'm your new security officer, I guess."

"You guess? You're not doing a very good job, are you Major?"

Then the Major lost his temper. "Nobody told me I'd be working with talking animals!

196

Nobody told me I'd be shot down by aliens! Nobody said anything about a swamp!"

Kongo stopped. He blinked at the irrational outburst. Then his hands began to curl into fists, and Tom Stroud knew that one swing of Kongo's fist could send the poor Major flying over the trees. "Kongo!"

Kongo turned and looked at Tom, his anger frozen. "Kongo," Tom said softly. "This isn't helping."

Kongo's anger suddenly fell away, as he returned to reason. "No, of course not. You're absolutely right. What do we do?"

But Ham was stomping impatiently from foot to foot. "I know what I'm doing. I'm gonna find Patty Cake." After a few bouncing steps, he lofted into the air and disappeared into the darkness.

"Ham! Come back here."

"How'd he do that?" Major Prescott said, staring after the flying chimpanzee.

Kongo shook his head. "That boy is impossible."

"This whole business is impossible!" the Major decided. Kongo turned to look at him. The officer was bedraggled and his uniform was ruined, but he held himself like a soldier. "Major, my apologies. I know you were trying to help my daughter and the others."

"We'll find your daughter, sir."

"Where are Mungo and Luna?" asked Tom.

"They went after the Amadorians. I tried to stop them, but..." said Laika. He sounded very tired. Tom shook his head.

"That does it. Now we have four lost animals. Nobody else leaves. We all stay together. Major, here's a Spysat map of the crash. Can you get us back to your plane?"

Prescott studied the map. "I think so..."

Kongo smiled at Tom and shook his head. "Didn't I say it? All of them, lost, within the first five minutes."

Twenty-two:
The Hunt for Patty Cake

The springs were noticably lower on the pickup truck as Kongo, Laika and the kids crowded in the back. Major Prescott and Tom were in the cab. Prescott gripped the wheel as if he was trying to find something real to hang onto. Tom Stroud laughed. "Cheer up, Major. You'll get used to it."

"I doubt it." After a moment he asked, "Are there many more of these…?"

"Zoonauts. We call them Zoonauts. About five hundred in total."

"Five hundred… Holy moly."

Tom glanced through the back window at Kongo, his huge worried face staring out at the swamp along the highway. "Yeah, that was my first reaction too."

In another part of the swamp, the storm had gone and a bright moon glistened on the water. Mungo and Luna made their way along; Mungo fluttering from branch to branch, Luna hopping from log to log. Mungo flapped up to the top of a lightning-split stump and craned his neck about.

"I can't see them."

ZONAUTS

"Well I can smell them. They're about a hundred yards ahead of us."

Mungo moved down to perch on a vine, which began to move, its head turning back to reveal that it was a snake, a large cottonmouth moccasin.

"Awwwk!" He quickly flew to a safer branch as the snake glided away into the water. Without thinking, Mungo shifted into Indiana Jones; "Snakes! I hate snakes!"

"Cute," muttered Luna.

"Be careful," Mungo whispered in his own voice. "This place is dangerous."

But Luna is sitting smugly on a log. "Dangerous? I come from a long and proud line of hunting cats…"

Then an eye opened on the log. It was not a log, but an alligator. Mungo flapped his wings in agitation.

"…Masters of the wilderness, experts in stealth and surprise…"

"Luna!"

The alligator opened its mouth, gobbled up Luna and dove beneath the water. A freaked-out Mungo beat his wings frantically, hovering over the spot where Luna disappeared.

"May-day, May-day! Officer down! Medic! Call Bay-watch!"

But nothing came from the depths but a few bubbles.

Under water, as the alligator sank to the bottom, Luna 'ghosted' out through the side of the beast, and paddled frantically upward. As she broke the surface, spluttering, and pulled herself up on a real log, she looked like a wet toilet brush.

"You're lucky you can do that," said Mungo, relieved. "You look like a drowned muskrat."

"Shud up."

"So which way now?"

Luna stuck her nose up and sniffed, then sneezed. "I tink dis way. Nod sure. Got mud up my dose."

Luna stalked off, followed by the flitting Mungo. What they didn't see was Ham flying by overhead, looking for Patty Cake.

Ham was watching the moonlit swamp intently as he weaved back and forth, quartering confusing patches of water and trees in a grid search pattern, hoping that he hadn't drifted off course. He could fly, but he wasn't good at it. Then he spotted the Amador ship on a small island.

"Excellent." He spiralled down to a landing next to the football-shaped ship. The door was open and red light was spilling out. Ham took a deep breath, remembering what had happened to the animals that the aliens captured, remembering Chuma and Bandit. He peeked inside.

Patty Cake was languishing inside a very strong cage. There appeared to be no door. "Great," she grumped. "Out of one cage, into another."

Ham appeared at the bars. "Patty Cake!"

Startled, Patty Cake banged her head on the top of the cage. Then she ran to the bars and kissed him. "Oh!"

Embarrassed, the two of them drew back.

"Oh! I, uh—I'm glad to see you." Patty Cake said.

Ham was grinning like a fool. He had finally gotten a kiss from Patty Cake. He was in heaven! "Yeah...heh heh...me too."

"Is my dad here?"

Ham suddenly thought that Kongo might be behind him and jumped back, badly startled. He looked around. "Where? Oh, you mean...no. I came alone. Let's get you out of there. Can you use your powers on the door?"

"There is no door. They welded me in. And the bars are too strong."

"I've got an idea," Ham said. "Don't go away."

Patty Cake shrugged, turned away, and shook the bars. "Where would I go?" Suddenly she heard a click, and the sound of something electronic powering up. Then Ham's voice came from behind her.

"Duck."

Patty Cake turned back, then threw herself flat as she saw Ham holding a laser gun that was too heavy for him. She clamped her hands over her eyes as he fired. "Noooooooo."

Patty Cake looked up. The bars of her cage were all melted off at different lengths. "Well, that was good," she said dubiously.

"Come on."

They paused in the doorway and peered out into the swamp. It looked peaceful enough until they heard Amadorian voices in the distance. "We still have to get the dog."

"Why? We got the monkey..."

"Gorilla. Because they want the dog. Luggage, remember?"

Ham and Patty Cake looked at each other. "I've got an idea," Patty Cake said, "There might be something to Sara's crazy dream after all.

ZONAUTS

Some distance away, Fishwick and Kornblend were slogging through the swamp. Fishwick stopped, his nasal stops popping in irritation. "What is that disgusting smell? What have you been eating?"

"Nothing! It isn't me! It's this swamp! It's gross!"

"The Amadorian Codex says—"

"Enough of the Amadorian Codex," Kornblend groaned. "I'm sick of hearing about it, and I'm sick of you."

"I'm going to request another sidekick," Fishwick complained grumpily. Just then headlights appeared in the swamp. Kornblend tapped Fishwick on the shoulder, almost knocking him over.

"What?"

"Look!" They peered at the headlights moving through the swamp. Fishwick rubbed his snout thoughtfully.

"This could be good."

Twenty-three:
Nose to Nose

The truck pulled up to the dock at the end of the road and stopped. Turning off the lights, Tom and Major Prescott got out, looking around with their flashlights, as the kids, Laika and Kongo hopped off the back.

Tom found Laika on the dock, sniffing the air. "Laika, can you find their ship from here?"

"I think so...but we're going to get wet." He trotted back to the shore and along the tangled tree roots to the end of the land. "Here goes."

Laika led the swimming, followed by Tom and Prescott shining their lights. Kongo brought up the rear with the kids riding on his mighty shoulders, as the little search party moved out across the water. Major Prescott was watching the murky waters with more than a little concern. "What about alligators?"

"I'll smell them before we see them," Kongo growled.

"Cool," said Cody

"Yeah, cool," the Major said, not completely convinced.

After about two hundred yards of wading, during which time they stepped more than once on things that slithered out from under them, Laika led them up onto a little island. He stopped.

"Do you smell that?"

"Alligators?" asked Major Prescott.

"Amadorians. Close." Kongo moved up and joined him at the front.

"Very close," he said.

"How do you know they're Amadorians," Jen asked.

"Because I know all of the smells of the swamp," Kongo said, "and that smell is not one of them."

"It's rancid," added Laika, "like old socks and garbage. Yes, close."

At that moment, Fishwick and Kornblend stepped out of the bushes, battle ready and each packing a laser. "Too close," Cody exclaimed.

"You try riding around in one of our ships for a few weeks and see how you smell," Fishwick snarled. Then, looking at Laika, he added, "And you will."

But Kornblend was more concerned about the drama of the moment. "Up against the wall, feet back, and spread 'em!"

Fishwick looked at him, trying not to explode. "   Will you PLEASE stop doing that?   He watches too much television," Fishwick said apologetically.

"Awright," Kornblend grumped.

But Kongo was losing patience. "Where's my daughter?"

Fishwick considered. "Ah, the other gorilla. Yes. Well, we'll give her back, if we can have the dog."

"What?"

"Forget it," Tom cried. "The US Government doesn't bargain with kidnappers..."

"Or aliens!" Jen added.

Kornblend turned his laser gun on Jen, "you'd make a tasty snack little girl! So watch it"

"Uh...yeah," Prescott added, trying to decide whether to go for his gun, but the two huge lasers in the hands of the aliens decided the issue for him. Then Laika stepped forward.

"No! I'll go. If you give back Patty Cake." He turned to Kongo. "Let me do this, old friend." Kongo looked stricken, not knowing what to do.

It was working. Fishwick and Kornblend grinned at each other. Medals would be theirs, and another stripe each. What they didn't see, behind them, was their ship approaching silently through the darkness.

But Kongo and Prescott had seen it. "That boy is impossible," Kongo muttered.

Through the cockpit windshield, Ham and Patty Cake were watching, as the ship's control levers moved by themselves. "How do you do that?"

Patty Cake shrugged. "I just imagine where I want the ship to be...and it goes, just like Sara's dream I guess. I don't know how it works."

"Well, I know how this works," Ham said, grabbing a microphone and moving a lever around to where he wanted it. The ship was now hovering right behind the Amadorians, its big laser cannons pointing directly at them.

"Time's up," Fishwick announced. "What do you say?"

"Drop them irons and reach for the sky!" boomed the ship's loudspeaker. Startled, the Amadorians did just that, then turn to see their own ship covering them with lethal intent.

Kornblend shook his head in amazement. "Wow! These Earth creatures are tough."

"Shut up luggage face!" hissed Fishwick.

Major Prescott was also impressed. "These are some funky animals."

"Zoonauts, Major," Kongo corrected him. "What shall we do with these miscreants, doctor?"

Fishwick swished his tail about angrily. "Let us go, or there'll be an invasion fleet here in twenty minutes."

Kornblend looked surprised. "There will?"

Fishwick shook his head. "Just once, read the updates we get from headquarters." Then, to Tom and Major Prescott. "You see what I have to work with here?"

"An invasion fleet?"

"Yes, in ten minutes" said Fishwick. "Big fleet. Lots of ships. Boom! Boom, boom, boom."

Tom and Prescott looked at each other. "He's bluffing," said the Major.

"Maybe, but I can't risk starting an interplanetary war just to find out." Tom looked at the two oversized lizards. "All right, we'll let you go this time, but stay off this planet, or the next time you won't be so lucky."

"Yeah," Cody piped up. "And get outta Dodge!"

Kornblend shook his fist. "Until next time! It ain't over till we say it's over!"

"Enough!"

Ten minutes later, both the humans and animals watched as the Amadorian ship streaked into the night sky. Prescott turned to Cody. "What was all that about luggage?"

"Who knows? Ya know, the Amadorians don't seem too bright to me. Do you think they're all like that?"

"And why didn't they just blast us when they got their ship back?" Major Prescott asked.

"Maybe they were under orders not to," said Tom.

"Or maybe their targeting computer doesn't work," said Ham, passing Major Prescott a handful of computer chips.

"I'll be darned."

"What did we miss?" Mungo asked as he and a bedraggled Luna shuffled into the light. Ham was standing close to Patty Cake, who had her arms around Kongo. Prescott looked at Tom, who shrugged.

"Apparently everything," Laika said.

Patty Cake looked at her father. "Can we go home now? I want to thank Sara for her dream. We couldn't have saved you any other way."

"I think that's an excellent idea."

Major Prescott was looking up at the ship, dwindling like a star in the sky. "I'm glad that's over."

"Oh, they'll be back," said Tom.

The Secret of Animalville

"Yeah. it's just a matter of when," Laika said thoughtfully. "But now, lets head on home. I'd like to see my new son."

This concludes the first story of the war between Amador and Earth.

Many of the animals helped.

Hsing-Hsing and Ling-Ling the Pandas gave us information on the Amadorians and their planet.

Horace the Owl, Mungo the Parrot and Laika the Dog did most of the writing, with Jen and Cody helping to make it 'cool.' Dr. Tom and I did most of the editing. The animals and humans who were there told us their stories.

We want the stories of the War with Amador to be read and enjoyed by both children and their parents. We also want people to understand that these dangerous space aliens are out there. Be ready for their next move, which could happen at any time.

ZOONAUTS

Twenty-four:
Methuselah's Last Word

The adventurers got home by midnight and all returned to what normal is for us. We made Sara an honorary Zoonaut. Of course, I was right to tell her the secret of Animalville. Her first dream already proved true and helpful. Who knows what might come of her dream of dangerous plants. told her, Record all your dreams, Sara, on a notepad by your bed. We dont know what will prove to be important. You should always listen to your dreams. They'll take you places.

The next few days, Air Force officers and investigators debriefed us. It was tedious as usual. Major Prescott got a tour of Animalville to meet all of us. Id like to say hes getting used to Zoonauts, but I think thats going to take a while. We are all helping him adjust.

We haven't heard much from Amadorians in three weeks. There hasn't even been one of their scout ships in orbit over Animalville. Maybe they're planning their next move. I don't think they've given up yet. Whatever they are planning, we'll be here to meet them head on, because we are Earth's first line of defense: Cody, Jen, Sara and all the special creatures of Animalville.

ZOONAUTS: THE SECRET OF ANIMALVILLE

Is the first book of a new and exciting adventure featuring the creative talents of Richard Mueller and Egidio Victor Dal Chele, brought together in print for the first time!

A young girl's tribulations at home and school are at the center of this fantastical tale. At first glance, Jen's troubles are typical of any eighth grader: teacher trouble, a know-it-all younger brother, and a gloomy conviction that her family is nothing like those of her friends. But her secret is deeper than anyone can imagine. Jen and her brother Cody are being raised with the help of a group of super-intelligent animals who watch over them and teach them things no other humans know. When Jen's English teacher refuses to accept her unusual family story as the truth, Jen confides in her best friend Sara about a crisis brewing at Animalville. Alien invaders threaten earth's inhabitants. Only cooperation among all sentient creatures on earth saves us all from disaster. The writer weaves themes of animal rights, ecology, and space exploration into this suspenseful story of Jen's race against time. Can Sara help?

BIOS

Richard Mueller is author of *Jernigan's Egg*, *Time Machine 24*, and *Ghostbusters: The Supernatural Spectacular*, which sold 150,000 copies. He has also written scripts for *Milo's Great Adventure*, *Buzz Lightyear of Star Command*, *Robocop*, *X-Men*, *Land of the Lost*, *Attack of the Killer Tomatoes*, and *Married . . . with Children*. He lives in Los Angeles.

Egidio Victor Dal Chele is known for his artwork in *God, the Devil and Bob*, *Scooby Doo and the Alien Invaders*, *All Dogs Christmas*, *He-Man & the Masters of the Universe*, *Fat Albert*, and *Shazam*. He lives in Los Angeles.

ZOONAUTS

ORDER DETAILS

Join the Zoonauts on their next adventure in China!
Join the *ZOONAUT CLUB* at :zoonautsfanclub.cjb.net
For Orders: 866-ZOO-NAUT(966-6288) or 800-484-7363

Published by Panda Print, the children's imprint
of Shangri-La Publications, Warren Center PA
or visit us at our URL http://shangri-la.Øcatch.com
ISBN 0-9719496-6-2 $14.95 US / $22.95 Canada

REVIEW

"Richard Mueller, author of Ghostbusters: The Supernatural Spectacular, X-MEN, and many other well-loved Hollywood successes, teams up with well-known artist, Egidio Victor Dal Chele, known for such artwork as Scooby Doo and the Alien Invaders and Fat Albert, to create a sure-to-be-a-hit book titled *ZOONAUTS: THE SECRET OF ANIMALVILLE.*

This book is a splendid mix of adventure and science fiction. It teaches the child reader about environmental issues and the importance of animal rights. Teamwork and the importance of goal setting are also subjects they will learn from this magnificent book.

This reviewer and her twelve-year-old son, Nicholas, thoroughly enjoyed this imaginative, fun, and winning book."

Jennifer LB Leese

***Children's Book Review* Columnist**